Dynamic Image Publications Presents

Loving You Blind

Christian Cashelle

Loving You Blind
By Christian Cashelle

ISBN-13: 979-8-9852060-4-3

Before you read Loving You Blind, read...

Move the Needle
The Last Bachelor Left

Other titles by Christian Cashelle

Ava's Story
When All Else Fails
My Mother's Child

My Joy
Gino's Revenge

Revisions of Life
Birds in the Rain

Stop Walking with Your Head Down - anthology co-author
Her Story, His Glory - anthology co-author
It's All Love - anthology co-author

Loving You Blind Playlist

Available on Apple Music

I've Changed (feat. Keyshia Cole) - Jaheim
Loving U Blind - Elle Varner
Kinda Love - Elle Varner
Say Yeah - Commodores
Where You Been Hiding - Sinead Harnett
Falling - Blxst
What You Think of That - Jaheim
CPR - Summer Walker
So Into You - Tamia
Lady - D'Angelo
About Him - Alex Isley
Alive (feat. Coucheron) - Kehlani
It Would Be You - Trey Songz
Take Care of Home - Dave Hollister
Girl Like Me (feat. H.E.R.) - Jasmine Sullivan
Hope - Jagged Edge
Be Happy - Mary J. Blige
Memories - dvsn & Ty Dolla $ign
I Don't Wanna - Jagged Edge

It's okay to not have it all together.
Love yourself, anyway.

chapter one

"I know Julian left you for dead, but I'm so glad you decided to keep the baby."

Nicole side-eyed her cousin, Raina, as she held a glass out towards her in a cheers motion. She wanted to knock the drink back in her face. Not only could she not enjoy a mimosa, Raina's comment made Nicole's stomach turn.

They were on their regularly scheduled brunch date after Nicole missed a few weeks in a row. Raina finally popped up to check in on her cousin and she confessed her current predicament. They decided against their usual spot and went to Wheelhouse STL downtown near the stadium. Nicole loved the brick walls and the natural light that came in from the large windows but it was a lot louder than she expected. There were two dj booths; one along the left wall and one on the upper level. They were seated near the one on the bottom while the other was empty. He played a mix of genres since the crowd was mixed. Raina seemed to love the playlist but she was also halfway tipsy. Nicole was a little jealous.

"My man, my man," Raina said, mocking the popular audio on Tiktok.

"Don't even finish that," Nicole said, stabbing her chicken. She ordered a southwest omelet instead of the steak and eggs she really wanted. Laying off of red meat. She'd read somewhere that was good for the baby.

"Too soon?"

"You're not funny."

"What? I'm just trying to lighten the mood. If you weren't going to be happy about the decision, why are you pro-life all of the sudden?"

Nicole slumped down in her chair and had to admit that Raina was right. She found out a couple of weeks ago that she was pregnant by her...well, technically Julian wasn't an ex...and had just come to terms with being a single mother.

Every possible emotion had filtered through her soul in the last three months. Nicole felt betrayed that Julian decided to go back to an ex who left him high and dry until his business became successful. She was hurt that her willingness to do whatever he wanted didn't give him any reason to commit to her. She was pissed that he didn't even try to stop her from quitting. She was conflicted by finally becoming a mother but knowing the father was in love with someone else. She was ashamed of becoming the statistic she'd always judged.

But what could she really do about it?

"You're right," she finally spoke. Raina's face lit up at the statement. "I chose to keep the baby so I have to make the best out of the situation."

"That's right!" Raina said. "And step daddies are always in season."

This time, Nicole laughed. She had no intentions of finding a step dad for her baby. She didn't even have intentions of the real dad being around, what good would another man bring?

"I don't want to deal with the real daddy let alone another one," she halfway lied.

"So when do you plan on telling him?"

Nicole bit her lip and shrugged. She honestly had no intention of telling him soon. She could almost bet he wouldn't be happy about it.

"Can we talk about something else?"

"Sure. When are you getting a job?" Nicole's stone expression made Raina slump down in her seat. "I'm concerned. Don't ask for some money soon. I have to save my coins to spoil the kid."

"I promise I won't," Nicole said. "I have some interviews coming up."

"Remote would be the best way to go."

Nicole sighed. "Raina, I really didn't come outside to have a lecture from you about my life choices. I'm actually done eating so we can slide..."

"These pregnancy emotions got you real sensitive." Nicole threw a rolled up napkin at her but Raina laughed as she asked the waitress for the check. She just told Nicole not to ask her for money but she told the waitress they were on one check. Nicole tried not to smile. "When's your next appointment?"

"Next week," Nicole said. "Get to hear the heartbeat again and possibly get some pics."

Raina slowly smiled, feeling the excitement radiate off of her cousin. "Well, let me know what is what. I have a shower to plan."

Nicole smiled at the thought. Up until then she hadn't really thought about the "fun" stuff expecting mothers get to do. The impending drama that was coming up in season 2 of her Julian story was sure to be full of anxiety, she had to promise herself that she'd enjoy her journey to motherhood as much as she could.

Should she take maternity pictures? Would Julian even be willing to take one with her? She'd love for her baby to have that photo, but was that realistic? How would it be when the baby actually came? Could she trust Tessica around her baby? Thinking about all these things suddenly made her feel sick.

"What are you doing the rest of the day?" Raina asked as they walked out into the daylight.

"I need to lay down for a little while before I get my place together. I'll call you later."

Raina nodded as they parted ways.

Her apartment was still when she returned from brunch. The usual kids outside had turned in for the day and Nicole was grateful for the peace. It had taken her some time to get herself together to leave the house earlier and now that her belly was full and her mind was a little less cloudy, she realized her house was a mess. Instead of getting right to it, Nicole decided to strip out of her clothes and take a nap first. She was only able to sleep a little while before the turning in her stomach woke her up. Her morning sickness hadn't been that bad but she learned that anytime she ate something this baby didn't agree with, it was sure to let her know.

After getting rid of her brunch, Nicole took a shower before coaxing herself into cleaning up. She went to her Tidal app on her smart TV, put on her favorite tracks, and cleaned her apartment. Just being in a clean space gave her a little bit more inspiration to get things done. Her first order of business was checking on the applications she'd submitted that past week. Of course, she wasn't smart when she quit her job. Unemployment did not cover resignations. She knew her little bit of savings would be gone soon, so she needed a job and fast.

Scratching her scalp, Nicole froze as a random memory of time spent with Julian resurfaced in her mind. She sighed, realizing just how many moments they'd had in that very room.

"I like your hair," he said, gently pulling a strand of it after she locked the door. Nicole's eyes widened as she pulled her hair back with her hands as if she was making a ponytail before letting it go.

"Thanks, I just took it down. I get it done tomorrow."

"You should wear it natural," he said. Nicole shrugged, moving around him to walk into her living room.

"It's too much work." He watched as she plopped down on her couch, different hair products spread out on her coffee table as a Pandora station played on her wall-mounted television. "What were you out doing?"

"At P's," he said, sitting on the couch next to her after taking off his shoes at the door. "They boring."

"So you hit me up, huh?" she asked, smirking. "I'm just as boring."

"I like being boring with you," he said, tapping her thigh.

Remembering moments like that made her feel less delusional. She hadn't imagined their connection, that was for sure. No one would convince Nicole otherwise. Yes, he never officially committed to her, but his actions never led her to believe that he wouldn't. It was a horrible feeling to know she'd missed the red flags she should have been paying attention to with him, but he was a great man on paper. He was a business owner. He was handsome. He didn't have any kids. He worked out. He liked to go out on dates. He was family oriented. They had fun together. The sex was good. Of course she wanted him.

And he had wanted her at some point. Their connection wasn't fabricated. It wasn't until Tessica came back that his affections changed. Nicole wasn't one to share a man. If he'd been on the fence and was so easily drawn back in by an ex, that was where he needed to be. That didn't mean it didn't hurt when he didn't choose her. It didn't make the rejection any less hurtful.

- Get a job.
- Focus on health.
- Take care of baby

That was the extent of Nicole's to-do list.

If it didn't have anything to do with those three categories, she didn't want any part of it. Thankfully, she'd gotten a few responses from some jobs she applied for and was waiting on next steps. Now, she was headed to her OBGYN to make sure all was well in baby land.

Her nurse practitioner worked out of an office off of Manchester. She'd been going to her for nearly a decade so when Nicole came in to verify her pregnancy, Dr. Adams reacted like a family member. Being a mother was always something Nicole wanted. She had to remember that despite her circumstances.

"Everything is still good," Dr. Adams said, coming into the room after her assistant took all of Nicole's vitals. "Weight gain is consistent."

Nicole rolled her eyes. "That's not what I want to hear."

Dr. Adams giggled. "Still wanted to lose weight? I know we talked about it before the baby came on board."

"Is that even okay now?"

She nodded. "Getting healthy is going to automatically drop some pounds. As long as the baby gets what they need and it's at a healthy loss of like 1 to 2 pounds a week at most you should be fine."

Nicole nodded. "Anything else I should worry about?"

"You don't have anything to worry about," Dr. Adams smiled. "Keep doing what you are doing and you and baby will be fine."

Nicole sighed in relief. "People make being pregnant over 30 sound so scary."

"It can be, but we won't worry about any of that unless we need to."

Feeling less anxious as she left the examination room, Nicole bumped into someone else coming to the back.

"Excuse me," she said, automatically placing her hand on her belly.

"No, that was my fault," the woman said. "I was on my phone."

"It's okay," Nicole said, trying to walk around her.

"Do I know you?"

Nicole frowned as she looked at the woman in front of her. She couldn't pinpoint her face so she shook her head.

"I don't think so," Nicole said, shifting on her feet. The woman bit her bottom lip before shaking her index finger.

"No, I do...you worked for Harris Trucking and Construction right?" Nicole slowly blinked. "I'm Deniece. Julian's sister. We met a few times."

Nicole's phone slipped out of her hand before sliding down to the floor. Deniece stepped back.

"Oh.."

"I got it," she said, leaning down to pick up Nicole's phone. "How are you?" she asked, while handing the phone back.

"G..good."

Deniece slowly nodded. "Well...it was nice seeing you."

Nicole silently cursed as she all but ran out of the doctor's office. St. Louis was way too small. Her palms began to get sweaty. Julian probably knew by now. Nicole was sure he probably got a phone call or a text the minute she left.

Maybe she wouldn't assume. Maybe she didn't realize it hadn't been that much time since Nicole quit. Maybe she didn't even know that Nicole and Julian used to be a thing. Nicole sighed in relief, choosing to believe the latter.

"What are the damn chances?" she asked herself while getting into her car. She hurried to get out of the parking lot, needing to put some distance between any connection to Julian and herself. All the while, carrying the most important one.

Nicole had only interacted with Deniece a few times. From what she would remember, Julian and Pierre always talked about Deniece not having much ambition and staying with her and Julian's parents. While he was planning their parents' anniversary party, Nicole remembered him complaining that his sister hadn't been holding up her share of the party planning duties. Nicole often found herself helping when they had downtime since he was so stressed about it.

chapter two

If Julian calling her several times was any indication, Deniece was definitely a snitch. It had been two days since Nicole had seen her at the doctor's office. Julian began calling that night and he didn't seem to be getting the hint, so Nicole finally answered the phone.

"Who is this?" she asked.

"Nicole." She closed her eyes at the sound of his voice. It hadn't been long enough. "You know who this is."

"I erased your number," she lied.

"But you remember my voice," he said. She didn't respond. "How are you?"

"Just ask me what you want to ask."

"My sister saw you. I didn't want to assume either way...but I just...you'd tell me right?"

"Tell you what?"

Julian sucked his teeth. "Don't do this dumb shit."

"What would I need to tell you, Julian?"

"If you're pregnant or not!" His tone rising caught her off guard. Nicole sat down at her dining room table, putting her phone on speaker and laying it down. "I know there's other reasons you could have been there but damn...just tell me. Are you pregnant? Is it mine?" That one made her frown. "How soon could we verify that? I'd need some time to sort things out but I could make it work..."

"Make what work?" she cut his rant off.

"...If you're pregnant and it's mine, of course we'd need to be a family."

Nicole blinked. "What do you mean, Julian?"

"Are you pregnant, Nicole?"

"I was there to confirm a pregnancy."

"And you're sure it's mine."

"Positive."

"Then we'll get married before the baby comes."

Nicole wasn't sure how much time had passed but Julian was still talking. She hadn't heard anything after 'get married' but she was sure it was all bullshit.

"Aren't you with Tessica?"

"...My family would come first, Nicole. She'd have to understand. It won't be ideal but..."

"Marrying me wouldn't be ideal?"

He sighed. "We haven't talked in months."

"You made your choice."

"You didn't have to quit the way you did."

"You made your choice!"

"None of that matters now. I'm not a man who doesn't take care of his family. Just having random ass baby mommas all over town. You know that ain't me."

Nicole's elbows hit the table as she leaned over to rub her temples. Her head was throbbing and she wanted him to shut up.

"Besides this proposal being wack as hell," Nicole said. "There's no need for all that."

"We don't really have a choice."

"I had one. And I chose not to keep the baby."

She wasn't sure why she lied but the silence afterwards almost caused her to take it back.

"I know you aren't saying what I think you're saying!"

"Don't do this dumb shit," she said, mocking his words a few minutes earlier. "You know what it means."

"How could you make that decision without me?"

"You've made plenty without me!"

"That's not the same thing and you know it!" Julian's tone was full of bass yet cracking at the same time. Nicole was confused. He couldn't possibly want a child with her. Why was he getting emotional?

"You don't want to be attached to me forever. Don't act like you do."

Julian groaned in annoyance. "It's not about what I wanted Nicole, it's about taking responsibility for what I did."

"Marrying me wouldn't be ideal. You don't want to be attached but would out of obligation. None of this sounds romantic to me."

"You're being childish, for real."

"Well, good thing you don't have to deal with my childish ass," she said, her finger hovering over the end button.

"Yeah, good thing. Would hate to have to raise a child with your mentality." Nicole's heart dropped as Julian ended the call first. Taking deep breaths, she tried to regulate her emotions but the tears were already falling.

"He thinks he's some type of prize!" she yelled, pushing her phone away from her and standing up. "Like being attached to him would be any better!"

Stumbling into the living room, she slumped down into the cushions of her couch, pulling her throw blanket around her neck. She bent her head down and screamed into the cover, aggressively wiping her tears. Nicole cried all she could until she eventually put herself to sleep.

Someone banging on her door while ringing the bell jolted her awake. There was no sun coming from the windows, so she knew she'd been asleep too long. Before she could figure out what was going on, the banging continued.

"I'm coming!" she yelled, struggling to unwrap herself from the cover. Once she was successful, she got up and jogged to her front door. Nicole sighed to see her aunt through the peephole.

"Hey Auntie," she said, swinging the door open. "Where's the fire?"

"Here apparently," Marie said, pushing past Nicole and into her living room. "Got your momma blowing me up to come check on you."

Nicole frowned. "Why?"

"She said you haven't been answering," Marie said. "Where's your phone?"

"I don't even know...last I saw it was in the kitchen."

"Well, go ahead and text her and then we'll talk about why your eyes are red and your face is all puffy."

Nicole groaned, scooting her feet across the carpet towards the kitchen. "Do we have to?"

"I didn't ask," Marie said. "I'll make some tea."

Nicole took a moment to compose herself after responding to her mother's text. They weren't super close, but Nicole knew not to ignore her for too much longer. They'd always clashed because their attitudes were similar. Nicole left when she was 18 and that actually salvaged whatever relationship they did have. They could have civil conversations, but whenever Simone went into "mother mode" Nicole usually tuned out. She was more inclined to ask Marie for advice.

"So, I'm sure she told you that I was pregnant," Nicole said after thanking Marie for the cup of tea.

"She did," Marie confirmed. "But I wasn't going to bring it up until you did."

Nicole sighed. "Between us?"

Marie side eyed her. "When does anything you tell me leave my lips?"

Nicole grinned and nodded in agreement. "I just lied and told the dad I got rid of it."

"And why would you do that?"

"He just tried to force a shotgun wedding on me."

Marie tried hard not to laugh but it came out anyway. "Isn't that what you wanted?"

"A marriage and two-parent household, yes? Someone to tolerate me out of obligation, absolutely not."

Marie nodded and sipped her tea. "So what's the plan then? You'll need his support to raise a child."

Nicole shrugged. "I didn't even plan to lie. It just came out."

"Do you want to be with him?"

Nicole sat and thought about that question. A few months ago, her response would have been a quick yes. There wasn't almost anything she wouldn't do to be his woman and build a life with him. However, Nicole was never one to double back. He humiliated her and dropped her as soon as his past came back. She would never be able to trust him with her emotions again.

"No," she finally answered. The look of doubt on Marie's face made her smile. "I'm serious Auntie. I don't spin blocks."

"I feel like I know what that means," she said. Nicole giggled. "So you really ready to be a single mom?"

"Is anyone ever really ready?" Nicole asked.

"I sure as hell wasn't," Marie said. Nicole sighed. Her aunt was one of the few in her family who didn't start out that way. She was married when she had Raina but it was over by her 5th birthday. "It won't be easy, Nic. I'll help as much as I can but this is still your responsibility."

"I get it," Nicole said. "I've been applying for remote jobs and hope to have one soon."

"You need one like yesterday." Nicole fought not to roll her eyes. "But I won't lecture you too much."

"Thank you."

The rest of her aunt's visit was pleasant. They began talking about possible baby names and other family drama that eventually kept Nicole's mind off of Julian's wack proposal.

chapter three

20 weeks. Nicole counted time in weeks now. Every important person in her life was aware of her pregnancy and, as she expected, there were mixed reviews. Her mother was happy to be expecting her first grandchild, but that didn't come without lecture. She hadn't told anyone else that she lied to Julian, so everyone figured he was just being a typical deadbeat. Every time Nicole showed them something she wanted for the baby or mentioned anything, they would try and force her to "call her baby daddy" and it was annoying. She was grateful that her aunt hadn't told anyone. She'd figure all that out later on. She'd gotten a remote job and although it wasn't in her field of study, it was ideal in her situation. She was doing remote clerical work for a rental car service and hoped to get into their HR department after her probationary period if a role presented itself.

Although she'd read horror stories about being pregnant in your 30's, she was doing okay at 33. She cut back on a lot of her dairy products and sugar. She'd been more active than usual; walking at least three times a week. She had also been looking into more holistic ways to give birth. She was determined to make this the best journey possible.

The only thing Nicole hated the most was being bored. She was used to working outside of the home, going out, doing bottomless mimosas on the weekend, and just dating Julian in general. She missed their conversation most of all and Raina gave her the bright idea to download a dating app.

"What do I look like trying to date right now?"

"Plenty of women do it," Raina said. "And I didn't say go out and do things with these men. You said you want some conversation right?"

Nicole bit her lip. "That's all it is?"

"Well, not for everybody," Raina said, laughing. Nicole rolled her eyes. "But you control what you want to do. Just get on there and take a look dang! Stop being scary."

"I'm not scared!" Nicole said, rolling her eyes. "I just..."

Letting her statement fall off, Nicole went to the app store and looked around on the dating category. "Do BLK," Raina said. "So you don't have to skip through so many outside the race."

"You know I'm all about black love," Nicole said, clicking the app and watching it download. "Do I tell them I'm pregnant?"

Raina sucked her teeth. "Girl no. That's not their business. Just have a normal conversation girl. Stop acting weird."

Raina snatched her phone so Nicole scooted closer to her on the couch so she could see what she was doing. She answered a series of questions and Nicole was shocked that Raina knew all of it.

"Okay cousin," she teased. "You know me a little bit."

"Shut up," she said, giggling as she pulled up Nicole's photos and picked 6. Nicole frowned at the few body pics that Raina chose.

"Those are old."

"Again...not their business," Raina said, hitting submit. "Now, I've been on here a little while too so if you find someone you like, give me their name first so I can make sure we ain't double dipping."

Nicole nodded as Raina handed her back the phone. "So what do I do?"

"You swipe until you see a pic you like, hit that little icon and it'll pull up more pics and a bio if they have it. If you like them, hit that button."

"That's it?" Nicole asked, scrolling through. "Oh, he's cute."

"Pass on him," Raina said, swiping the other way. "Immediately no."

Nicole laughed. "What happened with him?"

"Girl, he was trying to come to my house 3 minutes into the conversation. My guess is he's homeless."

Nicole laughed. "This ain't no good."

"Just have fun and get your conversation on."

Raina pulled her legs under her on the couch and began to flip through the Netflix category while Nicole scrolled through. She saw a few guys that she knew in high school and immediately blocked them.

"You don't have anything better to do on a Friday night?" Nicole asked. "You don't have to keep me company."

"I actually don't," Raina said. "The guy I was dealing with ghosted me."

Nicole frowned. "What? We liked him."

She sighed. "We did."

"Why do we have to go through this?" Nicole said, sucking her teeth. "It makes no sense how many good women I know are getting dogged out by..."

"I didn't say he dogged me out," Raina said.

"Being ghosted is definitely rude and disrespectful. All I see is men wanting this and that and wanting us to be this and that and they can't even communicate properly."

Nicole could feel herself getting upset. She closed the app and dropped her phone on the couch.

"No, get your conversation on," Raina said. Nicole giggled before putting her head on Raina's shoulder.

"Not tonight. Find us a good movie to watch."

The next few days while Nicole was in training for her remote job, she found herself scrolling through BLK. She'd matched with a few guys and although some conversations were started, a lot of them ended horrible before they even started. Many of them were straight forward, which she appreciated, but only wanted to talk about sex and hooking up. She was about to give up on her mini mission until she ran into one specific guy.

He immediately caught her eye because his smile was gorgeous and his dark brown skin was flawless. She was usually more attracted to clean cut men with fades, but his locs were neatly twisted at his scalp and falling from his head down past his shoulders. He was the only man she'd scrolled past that was fully covered, but in one of his pictures he had a muscle shirt on that showcased a neck and a right arm full of tattoos.

His profile name was Bap. Nicole frowned, hoping that wasn't his real name. She appreciated that his pictures weren't all shirtless in the mirror, taking a bottle to the head or throwing money around. One in particular with him on the beach looked like it could be a book cover or album cover. She was contemplating swiping on him.

"He probably won't even match with me," Nicole said before swiping right. Her heart dropped when it immediately matched.

That meant he matched with her before she did. "Oh crap…do I speak first then?"

Throwing caution to the wind, Nicole opened the message and tried to think of something interesting to say.

> *That's a dope picture on the beach.*
> *When's your album coming out?*

Pays attention, is funny AND beautiful.
You just made my day.

"Oh my gosh," Nicole said, rolling her eyes and blushing at the same time. She loved that he responded immediately. But what if that meant he just didn't have anything else to do? Nicole sighed before remembering what Raina said. That wasn't her business. She checked to make sure she wasn't missing anything in her training class before responding.

> *I appreciate you having something*
> *for me to pay attention to.*

You're welcome, love.

Nicole rolled her eyes. She wasn't a fan of pet names right out the gate. She considered that a strike.

What's the last book you read?

> *Look at you paying attention :).*
> *It was a book on human resources.*

(sleep emoji) What's the last fun
book you read?

> *LOL. That was fun to me.*

Be for real.

…You're right. I'll have to say Michelle Obama's biography then.

I'll take that one.

I like your vibe, Bap.
Let's get this out the way though.
Are you married or taken
(even if you don't think you are)?

Women just say anything lol.
No, I am not any of those things.

I have to ask.
Appreciate the honesty.

…You're not gonna ask me?

Nah…I don't feel like you the type
of woman to be on here if you were
spoken for.

Nicole wasn't quite sure what it was about his conversation, but this guy had her intrigued within just a few minutes. She imagined what his voice sounded like, if it matched his pictures. He seemed like a smooth talker but could keep up a conversation. Just what she wanted at the moment.

The rest of the day while she was training, Nicole and Bap chatted on the site. Nicole noticed that he hadn't moved to ask for her number or try to link up with her yet. It made her wonder if he was honest about not being attached to anyone. She had no room to judge, but she did not want to be having conversations with a married man or something who was taken. She could only take his word at face value for now.

What you doing, gorgeous?

Just finished training for my new job.

Wondering what's for dinner.

Congrats on the new job.

It's not much.
Just a work from home situation.

The way this world is right now.
Any income is major.
So congrats...like I said.

LOL you're right.
What's your first name?
I'm sure it's not Bap.

Rashaad, love.

How did you get Bap from that?!

LOL. Baptiste is my last name.

Creole?

Guilty. Don't put no stereotypes
on me though.

LOL. I won't.

The next few days went the same way. She trained for work while talking to Rashaad. He'd eventually asked for her number, but they hadn't spoken outside of texts yet. It was Saturday now, so she didn't have to work but planned to run errands and actually leave the house. To her surprise, she woke up with a voice message from Rashaad.

"Obviously this next step in our relationship is a big commitment." Nicole giggled at his humor. "But I felt as a man it was my duty to wake you up with something nice in your ear. So, good morning. Wake your ass up."

It was just as she imagined. The fact that his voice shook her was not lost on Nicole. She blushed all through her morning hygiene routine, wondering what to say back. It wasn't until she was dressed and inside of her car that she finally did.

"You are officially my alarm clock. Can't say I'm mad about it though."

When she didn't get an immediate response, Nicole pulled out of her parking space and headed on about her day. She was halfway through her errands when something changed the course of her day. The baby moved.

It was the first time it happened. At first, Nicole thought she was hallucinating, but it moved a little more. She was leaving the bank and had to hurry to her car before she started crying. This was one of the moments she'd been anticipating. It felt surreal because she never thought she'd be able to experience this feeling. As the years went by and her friends and family had babies, they tried to explain it but nothing prepared her for that moment.

It was bittersweet. She couldn't call Julian and tell him that his child was moving inside of her because he was under the impression there was no child. She'd have to experience this on her own and that was the choice she made. Her phone buzzed in her pocket, but instead of answering she turned the radio up and placed one hand on her belly as she drove home.

chapter four

Feeling her baby kick gave Nicole the motivation to continue to better herself. She was focused during training at work and made a point to journal and do some type of devotion every morning. At the moment that devotion looked like online sermons, but she had to start somewhere. It was hard getting rid of her distractions, but those baby flutters in her belly let Nicole know she didn't have any other choice. It kept her focused.

Until Rashaad's ringtone sounded.

It had been over two weeks since she matched with him and they talked every day. She had been evading his attempts to meet in person with a few lies. Covid. Work. Family emergencies. She could tell that he was getting frustrated, but Covid seemed to be the best defense. Although everything was open now and many people weren't wearing masks, including Nicole, there were still cases in the area. As far as Rashaad knew, Nicole was a huge germaphobe and had already suffered from the virus and didn't want to chance it.

She smiled at the mixed emotions that filled her heart as he called her as soon as she clocked out for lunch. It was a Facetime call. Heading into the kitchen, Nicole propped the phone up on her counter, angling it perfectly to make sure only her chest up was visible. When she answered, she had to bite her lip. He was outside, obviously working. His locs were pulled back into two flat twists and the sun made his brown skin damn near glow.

"Whoa," she said, placing her hand on her heart and smirking. Rashaad licked his lips and laughed.

"You a clown," he teased.

"You trying to start something," she said. He squinted a little before nodding.

"Been," he admitted. "You the one on weird time."

Nicole sighed, not responding because he was right. "You eat lunch already?"

He chuckled. "Waiting on the homie to come back with the order. What you got cooking?"

"Just some cabbage."

"Didn't you eat that yesterday."

Yes she did, the baby was craving it. "So...it's leftovers."

He nodded before shaking his head. "You busy tomorrow? Matter of fact, don't even answer that. Just make sure you ain't busy."

Nicole looked around the kitchen and sighed, leaning over on her elbows to get closer to the screen. "You really want to see me?"

"Don't play with me, man," he said, running his hand down his face. "You ain't trying to see me?"

"It's not that..."

"We can meet in the open at a park or something," he said, sensing her hesitation. "I'll bring some food. We ain't gotta touch." She couldn't help but smirk. He was the first man in a while who seemed genuinely interested in spending time with her. "I just want to see you...face to face."

Nicole got lost in his eyes. The way she could feel his energy even through the phone let her know that their chemistry in person would be crazy. She hated lying to him about why they couldn't see each other just yet. She honestly wanted nothing more than to see him. She could imagine his hugs. Rashaad had half a foot on her height, so she knew his frame would be massive compared to hers. Even with her thick frame, she just knew he could handle her. She could feel the security in his embrace already. She almost wanted that more than she wanted to kiss him. His full lips were one of her favorite features of his.

"I want that, too," she whispered. The smile that spread across his face made Nicole feel like a horrible person.

"So tomorrow then?" he asked.

Nicole gave him a weak smile before she lied. "Tomorrow."

"Cool, cool," he said, trying to hide his excitement. "I'll call you with the details later."

"Okay," she said, still speaking in a whisper now that she wanted to cry. "Have a good day at work."

"I will," he said. "Later."

Why did she have to meet him now? Why hadn't she met him before she got twisted up with Julian? Why was she quick to feel like this man was perfect for her? She didn't know him. They'd only been talking for a couple of weeks for God's sake. Why did she fall for men that quickly?

Nicole wanted to be upset with her cousin for talking her into downloading the app, but Raina told her to just enjoy the conversation. The problem with Nicole was enjoying the conversation meant being emotionally involved in it. Getting to know this man was not supposed to be part of the plan. How did she end up so invested?

She couldn't risk falling for him. Not this soon. Not with a baby by another man on the way. How would he even react to that? He probably wouldn't even talk to her anymore when he found out. It was better this way. Nicole bit her lip to control her emotions as she deleted her BLK account and blocked Rashaad's number in her phone.

"I better be crying because of you, kid," Nicole said, looking down at her belly before heading back to her desk, leaving her food in the microwave. She wasn't even hungry for her leftovers anymore.

Forgetting about Rashaad was the only option at this point.

chapter five

It had been awhile since Nicole set eyes on the building that housed Harris Trucking & Construction and it was a place she never wanted to be again. Now that she'd been away for some months, the cloudiness over her eyes had lifted. Realizing Julian was never into her the way she was into him was a hard pill to swallow. However, she knew she couldn't continue her lie for much longer. It wasn't fair.

Saying a quick prayer, Nicole killed her ignition before getting out of the car. She wasn't sure if the code would still work to get into the building, but she would try. Nicole froze next to her car as Julian walked out of the building. She was grateful that her car blocked the view of her growing belly before she had a chance to speak.

"What are you doing here?" Julian asked, stopping on the sidewalk. Nicole looked to make sure there weren't any cars coming since she was parked on the street.

"Came to talk to you," she said, clearing her throat to find some courage. He frowned while looking around the parking lot. It gave Nicole a moment to look him over and surprisingly, she didn't feel any of the old feelings she thought she would. He was still fine to her, that was a given, but the butterflies she used to get in his presence were gone. She honestly hoped it would stay that way.

"We don't have anything to talk about," he said, taking a step forward to cross the street. Nicole panicked, not wanting him to see her belly before she confessed.

"I lied about the abortion!" Nicole blurted out. Julian stopped in front of the hood of her car.

"What the hell you just say?"

She took a deep breath to try and still her heart. "I...I'm still pregnant."

His nostrils flared and his lips tightened when Nicole stepped forward enough for him to see the baby bump. Needing to create some space, Nicole took a step back and placed her right hand on the hood of her car before she cleared her throat.

"What?"

"We were arguing and I was upset that your sister was all in my business and I didn't like how you just assumed you could come back and run my life and then you made it about your relationship and you made being with me sound so horrible that I just wanted to…"

"You wanted to what?" Julian interrupted. "Hurt me?"

Nicole blinked. "I wanted to see if you would even care."

She knew Julian well enough to know that the way he just laughed meant he was not amused.

"What if I don't believe you?" he said. Nicole fought not to roll her eyes looking down at her stomach. "I won't assume because you gained weight that means my baby is there."

"I figured you would say that. I have a check up in an hour. You're more than welcome to come."

"Why are you just now telling me?"

"Because I'm past term to legally get an abortion."

Julian frowned at the accusation. "You're so damn childish. This is why I could never take you serious. You know I wouldn't have suggested it. Hell, I was pissed at the thought of you doing it."

Nicole felt nauseous with how angry she was. Granted, she was wrong for what she did but he was making her wish she never told him already.

"I don't know anything," Nicole said, dropping her arms to her side. "My doctor isn't far from here. I'll send you the details even though you should have them from your nosy ass sister." She backed up to the door of her car and pulled it open. "Figure out what you're going to do."

Nicole wasn't surprised when Julian walked into the office. However, she hadn't planned on speaking to him at all. She was already checked in and seated on the small two person bench facing the mounted television. He looked around for a moment before spotting her. She watched him walk over and sit next to her. Nicole wanted to get up and move but she fought against her instinct.

"You're unbelievable, you know that?"

She rolled her eyes. "Shut up talking to me."

"You don't get to be mad," he snapped. "You did this."

Nicole snickered. "Oh? I got myself pregnant? It wasn't you raw dogging every chance you got?"

Julian frowned. "Don't act like I forced you. You never complained about that."

She cursed inwardly at the feeling of getting emotional. "Julian, I swear...don't make me regret telling you." She watched as a vein almost popped out the side of his neck as he tried to regulate his own temper. Nicole's heartbeat was elevated so she took a deep breath before closing her eyes and taking another one. "I can't...I won't argue with you this whole time. I have to be careful....I am sorry that I lied," she mumbled. It took him a minute to respond.

"Has...has everything been okay up until now?" he asked after enough awkward silence passed.

She slowly nodded. "As expected."

"What does that mean?"

Nicole sighed. "No complications thus far."

"...Good," he said, nodding. "Good."

"Nicole Henderson?" Nicole got up as the nurse called her and Julian was right on her heels. "Oh, Dad is here today?" she asked. Nicole curtly nodded and walked past her into the back. "Dad, can you hold Mom's things while we get her weight?"

Julian nodded as he grabbed Nicole's purse and jacket out of her hands. She kicked her Crocs off and stepped up on the scale. Nicole hated this part. Even before her pregnancy began she was over 200 pounds. She wore it well, but she was very nervous about how she would spread in the next few months.

After the nurse got her vitals and situated them in a room. Nicole could feel a headache forming. Julian had been asking the nurse question after question. The nurse thought it was cute but Nicole was annoyed. She knew she made the right decision telling him but she was starting to regret it.

"When can you find out what the baby is?" he asked.

"A few more weeks."

"Do you have to wait until birth for paternity?"

Nicole had to close her eyes to keep her composure. She wasn't even sure if she was more upset about him asking or putting herself in this situation. All her life, she'd seen this story play out. Her grandmother. Her mother. Her aunts. Her cousins. Even some of her friends. Single mothers. Only a few of them didn't start out that way, but they all ended up that way. She never imagined this. She always thought she would be different. She'd be in a loving, committed relationship when she became a mom. It hurt. No doubt about it.

"Nicole, you can't be in your feelings about this."

"You don't get to tell me how to feel," she said, looking up at the ceiling. "We'll do it as soon as possible."

"You don't have to…"

"The sooner, the better. I don't want to look up 10 years from now and hear this shit ever again."

Julian threw his hands up. "Fair enough."

"I'm sorry," Nicole said, apologizing to the nurse. She nodded in understanding but did not respond. Nicole could hear Julian making noises as if he wanted to be acknowledged, but Nicole ignored him.

"So since this is my first check up," he finally said. "What did I miss out on?"

Nicole sucked her teeth as the nurse realized Julian's question was directed at her.

"Well, baby is growing well. We have some precautions we've asked Nicole to follow due to her age. It doesn't have to be a high risk pregnancy but we want to do all we can to make sure of that."

"High risk? What does she need to do?"

"I got it handled, Julian," Nicole whispered.

"I'd still like to know."

"I can give you the same information we gave her," the nurse said while looking at Nicole for permission. Nicole rolled her eyes but nodded. "Once we finish the examination, I will get that information to you."

"Thank you." After the exam, the nurse left the room. "Nicole."

"What, Julian?"

"You have to give me time to process this," he said. Nicole immediately felt bad for how she was acting. "You gotta know this is crazy. You told me you weren't pregnant anymore after not even telling me in the first place."

"I said sorry," she whispered.

"That doesn't make it any better. Then accused me of being a man that would talk you out of this…I just…I need a minute."

"…I wasn't sure what I wanted to do," Nicole admitted. "I needed some space to decide before involving you. I know that was wrong, but I was hurt when I realized we wouldn't be together. I really liked you, Julian."

Nicole caught herself getting emotional again. They never had this conversation before.

"I liked you, too," he said. "You know that. But honestly, we too grown to make these types of decisions on feelings, Nicole."

Nicole knew this pregnancy from here on out would be a roller coaster for her. She knew that Julian would be as condescending as he had always been, but it really hit different now. She hated that she had some type of connection with him before. She knew he liked her, that much was evident. He just liked Tessica more. Nicole told herself that she would stop beating herself up over Julian choosing Tessica. In reality it had nothing to do with her. She could say all of the things that she wished Julian had done differently, but if she was honest with herself, Nicole would have to take some of the blame. She should have never given so much of herself away. "You have to understand, Tess was it for me. At a very young age, I knew she was it. I never really took anyone serious after her. Not until you...but when she came back, all those old feelings just overpowered everything else."

"I don't need to hear this."

"I need to say it though," he said. Nicole huffed but did not respond."I didn't take you seriously because we were on different paths in life. You seemed content where you were and I wanted more."

Nicole frowned. She was far from dumb. She could read between the lines of what he was saying. Julian always used to make slick comments about her being loud on occasion, if her hair color was too loud or her nails were too long. She'd known as soon as she saw Tessica walking into the office that her more modest style was Julian's speed. Nicole wanted to believe their connection was strong enough, but it didn't have shit on history.

chapter six

Nicole bit her lip as she looked at her reflection in the mirror. It seemed as if everything changed overnight. She'd finally decided to loc her hair after months of debating and found someone in the city to do it for her. She sighed, hoping that she would stay with it. Her hair was a fine texture so she hoped it would get fuller as the months went by.

Her eyes dropped down to her belly that had also seemed to grow overnight. Almost 30 weeks in and she could honestly say she was looking forward to being a mother. After finding out she was having a baby girl last week, Raina was excited to plan a baby shower. Getting settled into her work from home job and getting ready for her baby girl were her only priorities.

Nicole rolled her eyes as a call from Julian disrupted her self-reflection. She didn't answer, but he called right back.

"You good? Y'all good?"

"All is well."

"...So you ignored me for what reason?"

"I'm not obligated to answer the phone for you," she stated, turning the bathroom light off as she walked out.

"You don't want me to check on you? If I wasn't calling I'd be a deadbeat right? Cut me some slack, please? Until we're sure of everything I want to be involved. I don't need any regrets."

Sure of everything to Julian meant being sure of the baby's paternity. He made sure to mention it just enough for Nicole not to forget it was a concern of his. It was comical to her. Julian knew good and well that when they were dealing with each other, Nicole was all about him. He had complete access to her. There wasn't any time or room for another man. However, she'd let him have his doubts for now. He'd be the one kicking himself in the end.

"I understand that, Julian. I already told you I'd keep you updated on anything I felt you needed to know. You gotta work with me on these early morning calls though."

"You work with me," he said. Nicole sighed.

"Okay. Whatever. We're good. Talk to you later."

Nicole hung up before he could say anything else. He immediately sent her a text calling her childish. She responded with the middle finger emoji.

Since her shower was in a few weeks, Nicole decided to get her first retwist. She was a little anxious about how it would look, so she wanted to get it now so she'd have a chance to do something different. She'd been eyeing a wig that would work for the look she wanted. It amazed her how much she liked her hair though. She was worried about the 'ugly stage' that so many women talked about, but Nicole loved her budding locs so far. She'd gotten in for an appointment to a well known loctician in the city. She wasn't able to have her start them, but she wanted to continue the process with her. She was so excited that she got there early.

"You started these when?" Maya asked, fingering through them. "Your hair is fine but they seem to be locing well."

Nicole smiled and sighed in relief. "Really? Good! I've been trying my hardest to keep my hands out of it."

"You did good," she said, spinning the chair to put her cape on. "You like the size and everything?" Nicole nodded. "Okay, well your scalp doesn't look too bad so we'll do a regular wash and style today."

Nicole's first retwist appointment went well. She had opted out of an updo and left it down. She hadn't been feeling her best the last few days, but getting her hair done and her eyebrows waxed made her feel less sloppy. Spring weather was breaking and it was pretty warm that day, so being able to wear a ¾ sleeve maxi dress was comfortable yet cute. She prayed that it didn't get too hot as her pregnancy progressed, but she didn't have much faith in St. Louis weather.

Leaving out of the salon, Nicole froze as she saw a familiar face in the parking lot. It was one she'd never seen in person before, but she had no trouble recognizing it. Hoping that he didn't see her, Nicole looked to the left and right to see the best way to get to her car without him noticing. She quickly stepped back behind the column in front of the salon. She tried to hit the button on her alarm so she wouldn't fumble with the door when she got to it. Nicole's heart dropped when she heard him laugh. He was closer than she thought.

"You don't gotta hide from me, gorgeous. I can take a hint."

Nicole jumped and turned to see him behind her on the other side of the column. She thought about lying but decided against it.

His brown eyes shined in amusement. "What's up, Nicole."

She sighed, breathlessly. "I just didn't want it to be awkward... Hi, um...."

"...Rashaad," he said, licking his lips while holding back a smile.

"Rashaad," she whispered.

"The locs look nice," he said, looking over her face. "It's a good look on you."

Nicole's arms fell to her sides. She gripped her purse to make sure it didn't fall out of her hands. She immediately wished she hadn't done so as his eyes followed.

He licked his lips while looking over her body. "I see why you ghosted me." He nodded towards her belly.

Nicole swallowed her nerves. "That's none of your business."

He threw his hands up and chuckled. "I get it, mama. I don't do drama anyway. You saved me the trouble."

Nicole rolled her eyes. "I don't care what you do."

Her attitude did not phase him. "You have a good day, Nicole." Rashaad walked away in the direction of the salon.

The way he said her name ignited a flame. Nicole wasn't sure if it was pure attraction or half annoyance, but she didn't like it at all. It had been almost two months since she ghosted him but she hadn't forgotten that voice. She pressed her hand to her cheek, hating how hot it felt as she managed to get to her car. All of their conversations came flooding back and her heart ached.

Those weeks they'd been phone buddies felt like a distant memory to Nicole. They hadn't even talked about anything in depth, having the most random conversations at any given moment. Nicole loved that she didn't have to force intellectual conversations with him just to feel smart, but she could also bring up a topic and he'd hold his own. Her belly shifted with movement as she rushed into her driver's seat and took a moment to still her heart.

It just wasn't fair to her. She tried not to be bitter from old relationships. She was open to a man leading. She kept herself up, as much as she could. Why wasn't she enough? Then to find a man who seemed to think she was, only to not be able to have him because of her dumb decisions in the past. Nicole didn't know how many more times love would slap her in the face for believing in it, but she didn't have any real fight left.

chapter seven

Two weeks after her shower, Nicole had a baby girl at 38 weeks pregnant. The time between them had gone so fast, she wasn't sure what day it was anymore. Surprisingly, when she called Julian to tell him she'd gone into labor, he showed up almost immediately. Her labor wasn't quick. Her aunt, mother ,and Raina were there, but Nicole really only wanted her aunt in the room. That caused a little bit of an argument, especially since Julian stayed, but Nicole didn't want the guilt of him not being there on her mind. If he chose not to be, that was on him. She would never be the reason her daughter didn't have a relationship with her father. She'd already instructed the nurses and doctor that Julian wanted a paternity test so she didn't have to deal with it once she had her.

Sylar Renee was her name. Against her family's wishes, her daughter's last name was Harris. Julian seemed to have disappeared the rest of the day, but a nurse informed Nicole that he'd been in front of the nursery whenever Sylar was present.

She had to admit she had mixed emotions. She was a mom and that took precedence over any other feeling. She'd waited her whole adult life to be one. She admitted to almost giving up on the idea of having a baby. It made her feel guilty for not being 100% about it in the beginning, but she always wanted a family more than anything. The reality of being a single mom hadn't been tangible the whole pregnancy. Now she really had an innocent child depending on her. She contemplated on whether she should have taken Julian up on his shotgun wedding offer. Would it be better for Sylar to be in a two-parent household? Would Julian be in her life full-time once the test confirmed what she already knew?

Nicole wanted to be bitter, but she was exhausted from fighting the situation. She had no one to talk with about her mixed feelings, but she'd finally decided that holding on to her feelings for Julian was a lost cause. Wanting someone who would only be with you out of obligation was bound to be a worse alternative. She'd seen how that played out in her family.

Speaking of family: Nicole's had gotten on her nerves the duration of her labor. She was sure that her daughter would look just like her grandmother. Nicole never spent a lot of time with her mother, but the days leading up to her delivery, Simone decided to come stay and get her place ready. Nicole didn't have much room in her apartment, so Simone spent most of it complaining about her needing a bigger space. It wasn't as if Nicole wasn't aware, but she could only afford what she could afford. That led to another suggestion of Simone's that Nicole wasn't trying to hear.

At the moment, she was fussing over the blanket that the nursery had wrapped around the baby while Marie was brushing Nicole's new growth down and putting her locs into a bun.

"Please get your sister out of here," Nicole mumbled. Simone sucked her teeth.

"I can hear you."

"Leave her alone before she wakes up."

"You ain't been a mother for two seconds and already irritated with your own baby?" Simone said, smirking. Nicole frowned.

"Now how you get that from what I said?"

Raina walked in with a bag from Shake Shack. "I got your food," she sang in a tone that let Nicole know she was trying to diffuse an argument before it even started. "Eat up while it's hot."

"You need to be trying to see what the test results are," Simone said. Nicole rolled her eyes as Raina pushed the tray over her lap and she tore the bag down the middle.

"I already know the results. Her daddy is the one who needs to find out."

"You could make it easier on him."

Marie situated the bun and kissed the side of Nicole's head. She smiled up at her in appreciation and tapped Raina with her foot who was sitting at the end of her hospital bed, sneaking fries off the tray.

"You're going to need his support raising this pretty baby."

Simone kept ranting, but Nicole distracted herself by looking at her daughter. At least her mom was right about that, she and

Julian made a pretty baby. Nicole always knew they would. These circumstances weren't in her fantasy though.

Marie finally got Simone to agree to leave with them, so Nicole got the next few hours alone with Sylar. She was sure she'd send her to the nursery to get some rest, but when they came for her, Nicole declined. Her little coo's and her newborn scrunch were the highlight of Nicole's life. Even though she slept most of the time, Nicole found herself committing everything about Sylar to memory. Her honey colored skin and her little flat nose. Her long fingers and toes and the birth mark on her leg. She snuggled with her as much as she could while she didn't have to share.

A few hours later, Nicole watched Julian as he walked back into her hospital room. She'd known she would see him that day. She and Sylar were scheduled to leave in the morning, but the nurse had come about an hour ago with the paternity test results. She sighed, watching him walk in with the weight of his actions on his shoulders almost made Nicole feel bad for him. Deep down, she knew that he'd known all along. It was the only reason she hadn't gone off when he suggested it. She wouldn't lie and say it didn't hurt…but hurt her was something that Julian did well.

Nicole sighed before going back to putting lotion on her thigh before pushing her gown back down. She grunted, her core still in pain, hoping she hadn't shifted the pad that was protecting her from any leaks.

"Do you need help?" he asked. Nicole shook her head but did not look his way. "Who is coming to get you tomorrow?"

"My mom. Sylar will be in soon."

Julian waited until Nicole was laid back on the bed in a more comfortable position. "Thank you for being so calm about this… I."

"I didn't do it for you," she said, cutting him off. She typed away at her phone before putting it in her lap and looking at Julian. "All of my life I've seen this scenario play out. My momma, my aunts, my cousins, my friends…always some baby daddy drama. Always begging a man to be a father. Always bitter and stressed out. I didn't want to have a broken home."

"I tried to fix that…"

"No, you tried to sacrifice yourself to seem noble. I don't want a broken home, but I will not be in a loveless marriage."

Julian closed his mouth and nodded.

"I can't have what I wanted, but I can give my daughter and me peace."

He realized she stopped. "What does that mean?"

"Now that you know she's yours, I'm giving you a choice. You have an out. I won't beg you, chase you or bother you if you decide being part of her life is not what you want. Or you can sign her birth certificate...but if you choose that option, know that you are choosing to be an active father, a consistent father and we'll be all good."

"Just like that?" he asked. Nicole swallowed the lump in her throat.

"Just like that."

"My family is down at the nursery," he said. Nicole looked up at him but didn't respond. "I wanted them to see her when I did, but I...wanted to make sure you were okay with that first."

"Who all is here?"

"My parents, Deniece and P."

Nicole sighed but nodded. "They can come in."

Julian jumped a little as the nurse rolled the bassinet in. Nicole smiled as she saw Sylar's feet kicking.

"She's up and ready to eat, Momma," the nurse said.

"Go wash your hands," she said to Julian as the nurse handed Sylar to her.

"Don't talk to me like a kid," he frowned, but walked over the sink. Nicole rolled her eyes as the nurse giggled.

"I'm going to let him feed her, but can you tell his family down at the nursery they can come in a few minutes?"

The nurse nodded as she left. Nicole kissed Sylar's nose before gently rocking her. "There are bottles in that drawer." She nodded towards the bassinet.

"Why aren't you breastfeeding?" He asked as he pulled the drawer open.

"Because she's going to be in two different houses. Or would you prefer not to keep her until she can eat solid foods?" Nicole snapped. Julian's nose flared before he looked down and read the directions on the bottle. "Do you know how to hold a baby?"

"Nicole, don't piss me off."

She tried not to smile at her victory. If he could say ignorant stuff so could she.

He stepped closer to take Sylar from her and she carefully situated her in his arms. She fussed a little but he sat on the edge of her bed and gave her the bottle. Nicole sat up and took a picture with her phone.

"She really looks like a doll," he said. Nicole cheesed before scrolling to a photo album she'd already made.

"I know right? Look at this picture from earlier? She's so stinking cute. I can't wait for her newborn pictures."

Julian chuckled but kept his attention on her. A few minutes later, there was a knock on the door. Nicole could see Joyce peeking through the door and she laughed.

"Come on in, Miss Joyce."

"Come meet your granddaughter and niece," Julian said, still not looking away from Sylar. Nicole watched as they went to wash their hands and then crowded around Julian. She appreciated that they all had masks on. At least she knew that when Sylar was with them she'd be protected.

"I can't believe y'all got a kid," Pierre said, shaking his head.

"Tell me about it," Nicole said. "How's Sage?"

"She's mad she couldn't come. We didn't want to bombard you though," he said.

"I appreciate that, but next time you visit make sure she sees how cute my baby is," Nicole joked.

"What's her name?"

That came from Deniece, who had been quiet since she came into the room. Nicole wasn't too fond of her still, but the joy of being a mom overshadowed her desire to be petty.

"Sylar Renee," Nicole said, purposely leaving off her last name just because she knew that was the real question.

"How are you feeling?" Joyce asked. Nicole smiled, sheepishly. She had met his parents before in a professional setting. At the time, she had only just started working for them so nothing with Julian had transpired yet. It was a little awkward to go from that to this, but Nicole knew everyone in that room was excited about the baby.

"We're both good. Ready to go home in the morning."

"Please let me know if you need anything," she said.

"She won't," Julian said. "But I will."

Nicole rolled her eyes. "Shut up and let her hold her grandbaby."

chapter eight

Three months postpartum. Nicole felt more like herself than she had in awhile. It wasn't even her old self, but a better version. She had no idea being abstinent and focusing on herself would change her mindset so much. It was a struggle with a newborn, but thankfully Julian stepped up and co-parenting hadn't been that bad.

Up until then, Nicole hadn't been too focused on losing baby weight, but she and Raina decided to join a local gym together for accountability. She picked one that had a daycare to make it more accessible to her. No excuses. It was also a way for her to get out of the house since most of her days were spent inside.

The gym wasn't huge but it was clean and never that crowded. It was funny to see how most of the women stuck to the cardio equipment while the men dominated the free weights side. This was the first time Nicole had gone by herself. Raina said she had something else to do but Nicole thought she was just being lazy that day.

Knowing that Sylar would be hungry soon, Nicole did a cardio workout for about 45 minutes before calling it a day. She almost stumbled over her own feet when she turned and saw him walking towards her.

She hadn't seen him since that day in the hair salon months ago but he was still fine. Skin still flawless. Muscles still flexing. Smell still intoxicating. As soon as it filled her nostrils, Nicole knew he was too close.

"Hey gorgeous," he said, smiling. "I see that congratulations are in order?" Nicole frowned but he pointed to her stomach. "My bad...I didn't want to assume..."

She smiled. "No. Yes, she's here. Thank you."

He nodded and licked his lips. "Baby girl huh? That's what's up. You seem happier than when we last ran into each other."

"Who would be happy to run into someone they ghosted?" Nicole teased. They both laughed. "It's nice seeing you, Rashaad."

Nicole was sure he had to stop licking his lips and eyeing her like he was in the middle of the gym before she jumped on him. "I'm glad you remember my name this time, Nicole."

"I didn't forget it last time," she confessed in a whisper. "I was just..."

"I get it," he said, nodding while his bottom lip disappeared between his perfect teeth. "Under different circumstances, right?"

Nicole was breathless. A lot had changed for her since she had Sylar. Before she wasn't even thinking about men but now she couldn't lie and say she didn't want a relationship. It was just hard to believe anything any of them said. They did what was convenient for them and didn't care about anyone else. Nicole didn't have the luxury to play that game anymore. She had a child to protect.

"I get it," Nicole said with a polite smile. "You aren't step dad material." Rashaad chuckled and she frowned. "What's funny?"

"I never said that."

"Yes, you did."

"I said I don't do drama, that's just how you took it."

Nicole closed her mouth and Rashaad chuckled. He reached up to push one of her locs from her face, letting his hand slide down her cheek and neck. Nicole felt her skin burning under his touch. She bit her lip and stepped over to the side, making his hand fall. He smirked before nodding in acknowledgment.

Nicole used her speechless moment to really take in Rashaad. His hair had grown since she first swiped right on that dating app. She could tell that his time in the gym was a commitment, because the muscle definition in his arms was definitely popping. She sighed, suddenly thinking of those gym couple videos she'd seen, sweating with him would be an experience...

"Her daddy involved?"

"Huh?"

Rashaad leaned in closer and Nicole held her breath. "Is her daddy involved?"

"Yes," she breathed.

"Hit me up when it's momma's day off."

Nicole's mouth dropped open as he walked off. She couldn't help but laugh and roll her eyes.

Nicole picked Sylar up from the gym's daycare and headed home. Sylar had fallen asleep in the car and Nicole was scared to move her out of her carseat, so she brought her into the bathroom and sat her next to the tub as she ran herself a bath. Although it had been three months, Nicole felt like she was always on pins and needles when it came to Sylar. All of the articles and books she'd read while pregnant felt like a waste of time. Nicole had no idea what she was doing and although Julian was involved, Nicole struggled to find the balance.

Working from home had been a saving grace as far as daycare was concerned, but that meant she never got a break. Sylar's cat naps weren't long enough for her to get anything done or rest herself and she tried not to wear out her welcome with Marie. While soaking in the tub, Nicole looked at her sleeping baby and wondered what their lives would be like. She prayed they would be closer than she was with her mom.

"I'll make sure you can talk to me about anything," Nicole whispered before leaning her head back against the tub wall and closing her eyes. Her doorbell ringing caused her to splash water and almost slip under in the tub. She looked at Sylar frowning before she began to cry.

Nicole silently cursed as she sat up to drain the tub, getting out and grabbing her towel. She quickly dried off before throwing her robe on and picking Sylar up out of the carseat. Shuffling into the living room while also trying to calm her baby, Nicole blinked a few times to make sure she was seeing clearly through her peep hole.

"What are you doing here?" she asked.

"What's wrong with her? Let me in."

Nicole sighed before swinging her door open and letting Julian in. He immediately took Sylar from her and kissed her cheek. "Hey princess, why are you in here fussing?"

"She just woke up," Nicole said, shuffling to the kitchen to make her a bottle. "Why are you here?"

"My daughter lives here."

"Julian, why are you here unannounced?" she asked, frowning at him as he walked into the kitchen, Sylar's cries were now a little softer, but she was still fussy.

"Nicole...my daughter lives here."

Because she was exhausted from the day, she finished making the bottle and handed it to him before walking to her bedroom and closing the door. She knew she'd have to have a conversation about boundaries with Julian soon, but she was afraid it would keep him from being active. He was always available for Sylar, he even took her to the office a few times. They didn't have any legal agreements in place but that was because they had been amicable up until this point. Julian sent money on his own and often asked if anything was needed. Sylar had everything she needed at his place and Nicole rarely had to send her with a bag. She didn't want to deter him from being a good father, but now he was pushing it. Showing up unannounced let Nicole know he thought he could do whatever he wanted and that was not the case.

However, she took that opportunity to go back to the bathroom and do her much neglected skincare routine. Once she was settled and realized how late it was, she went back into the living room to see Julian spread out on her couch with Sylar asleep on his chest. She took a picture and sent it to his phone before dropping her phone back into the pocket of her robe. She gently reached for Sylar and Julian tightened his grip. Once he opened his eyes and saw Nicole, he let his hands fall on the couch. Nicole cradled Sylar against her chest, kissing her curls as she walked her back into the room and settled her into her bassinet near her bed. After making sure she was asleep, she went back into the living room expecting to lock the door behind her baby daddy. She laughed to see him still on the couch.

"You are too comfortable," she said, slapping his arm. "Get up. It's time to go." He groaned before slapping her hand away. "Julian...you have to go."

He opened one eye and looked at her. "Why? You got a man coming over here? You better not be doing shit with my child in the same room."

Nicole bit her lip to keep her laugh in but it came out anyway. "Don't you have a woman? Who I'm sure wouldn't be okay with you sleeping on your baby momma's couch at ten at night. Get the hell up!" Her amusement turning into anger. "And don't question me about anything I do."

Julian chuckled as he sat up and ran his hand down his face. "You're funny trying to bring her up. She knows I'm spending time with my child."

Nicole rolled her eyes. "Julian, I truly don't care what you and Tessica got going on. Your daughter is sleeping so goodbye. I'll drop her off to you this Friday as planned."

Julian looked as if he wanted to say something else, but Nicole walked off towards her front door. He chuckled before grabbing his phone and keys off the coffee table and walking towards the door. Nicole hurried and locked it once he was finally out.

chapter nine

He always smelled so damn good.

Even when they crossed paths at the gym, Nicole couldn't help but inhale whenever she was around him. Every sense she had tingled at his scent alone. She could only imagine what adding his touch would do to her system. It scared her to even think about it.

It has been a couple of weeks since she first ran into him at the gym, but now it happened all the time. She wanted to say he was stalking her, but they hadn't been friends on social media for him to see her location on her private page. Nicole had to admit that she anticipated seeing him, listening to his smart remarks and smelling his scent...even after he worked out. She was waiting for her cousin on the treadmill when the smell invaded her senses. She glanced at him standing on the machine to the right of her before pulling her ear bud out of her ear.

"What you say?"

"Don't slim down too much," he said. Nicole frowned, looking up into his eyes in question. "Your weight, love."

Nicole huffed. "I'm not doing it for you."

"Really? I could have sworn you were," he teased, licking his lips. "That's my narrative anyway."

Against her will, she laughed. "Always a slick remark with you." Nicole hit stop on the machine, grabbed her water bottle and jumped off. Rashaad followed suit as they headed in the direction of the locker rooms.

Rashaad winked at her. "It makes your gym experience more enjoyable. You know it does."

Nicole absentmindedly nodded, shocking them both. Rashaad recovered before she could by stopping her from working further.

He stepped in front of her, moving closer into her personal space. "Is it momma's day off yet?"

The scent was too intoxicating at this point. Nicole felt her ears ringing and she just knew this man would be trouble. The passion in his eyes as he roamed her body wouldn't allow her to run just yet.

"To...tomorrow is momma's day off," she whispered, staring at his lips. She gasped as she felt him touch her hip, taking a few seconds to realize he was removing her phone from the pouch it was in. She watched him as he tapped the screen, turned it around to use her Face ID before tapping away at it again.

"Deleted or blocked?" he asked.

"...Blocked."

He tapped away before smiling a few seconds later. Nicole assumed he called himself since his phone lit up in his other hand.

"Can you spend it with me?" Although it was framed as a question, Nicole knew that it wasn't. "What time are you free? 5 or 6?"

Her head was spinning at this point. It was pitiful that a gesture as simple as making a plan had her ready to ask this man to marry her.

"Um...6 is good."

Rashaad smiled. "I'll call you in the morning to iron out the details." All she could do was nod. He chuckled at her sudden loss of words and leaned in to kiss her cheek. "Enjoy your day, love."

She was still stuck until Raina rounded the corner of the locker room and pushed her. "Girl, get yourself together! You can't let that man see you sweat like that."

"He can see me do whatever he wants," Nicole said, fanning her face and leaning into Raina. They both laughed before heading over to the stairmasters.

"I just know you weren't falling over that man and don't know him," Raina said, stretching out her leg before hopping up on the machine. "So spill it."

Nicole sighed. "Remember when you made me download that app?"

Raina sucked her teeth. "I didn't make you do anything. You were bored and lonely."

"Well anyway," Nicole said. "We vibed but he kept asking me to meet. So, I ghosted him," she said, keeping it simple. "But I've run into him a few times here."

"Oh, that's why you're trying to get slim thick!" Raina said. Nicole rolled her eyes.

"No, I'm getting healthy for me and my child," she said. Raina waved her off. "He just seems arrogant."

"The way you were about to faint I'd say he has reason to be," Raina laughed. "He's not your usual type. I love that for you."

Nicole rolled her eyes before starting her machine. "Let's just see how this date goes before you go marrying me off."

The two finished their workout before Nicole headed to the daycare to pick up Sylar. She was glad she was asleep by the time she got home so she could shower in peace. Julian would be picking her up in the morning so Nicole got her bag ready and packed so she wouldn't have to do it in the morning. Sylar was up and hungry by the time she finished.

"Hey hungry girl," Nicole said, picking her up and kissing her face and neck. Sylar cried harder. "Oh no, hurry up Mommy!" Nicole secured her between her side and her arm before moving out of the room towards the kitchen to warm a bottle up. While preparing it, her phone went off. She still had her ear buds connected, so she double tapped them before going back to what she was doing.

"Hello?" she asked.

"It's Rashaad."

Nicole almost dropped the bottle at the sound of his voice in her head. "Oh…hey."

He chuckled. "You busy?"

"Feeding baby girl," she said. "I thought you were calling tomorrow?"

"Couldn't wait," he said. Nicole blushed. "Wanted to make sure you weren't going to flake on me."

"Is there a reason I should?"

"You're the one acting scared." Nicole decided not to respond. "Do you have any food allergies?"

"No."

"Any physical illnesses I should be aware of."

Nicole giggled. "You trying to go hiking or something?"

"I'm putting a plan together. Just wanted to make sure you'd be comfortable."

"You're not gonna ask me what I want to do?"

"I got this."

Nicole exhaled as she looked down at her daughter. It wasn't fair that every time this man talked to her, he debunked her usual type with the most simple statements. She felt herself getting soft again and she halfway hated it.

"I appreciate you planning a date," she said in a lower tone.

"Your appreciation is noted but that's what I'm supposed to do baby," he said. "I'm a grown man."

Nicole hummed involuntarily. Rashaad was definitely a grown man. From the moment she saw him, he pulled a certain energy out of her. It was calming, like Nicole didn't have to do anything for their attraction to thrive. It was an underlying current that fueled their interactions but didn't overpower it.

"I'll let you go but I'll send details tomorrow. Can I pick you up or would you rather meet there?"

"I can meet you," she whispered. Rashaad chuckled.

"Can't wait."

By the time she woke up the next day, Nicole had a confirmation text with an address on where to meet Rashaad at 6p. She thought it was a little early for a date, but given that he didn't say it would be at night time, she'd go along with it. She sent him a message asking how she should dress. He replied that he knew she was fishing for more information but told her that casual was fine. Nicole sucked her teeth at her failed attempt but got up to look for the perfect outfit anyway.

Fate aligned for her with Julian picking Sylar up the night before, so Nicole took her time that day. She did a workout video at home, very happy with the fact that she could commit to it before lounging around and catching up on her favorite shows. She made sure to set an alarm to get ready at 4:30. Having locs definitely helped cut down on her prep time, but she wanted to make a good impression. The first one being her running away from him while pregnant; Nicole felt she owed him her best. The look on his face when she exited her car was well worth it.

"On time and looking this good?" he asked, opening the door for her. "I did something right in my past life."

Nicole blushed. "I'm cute?" she teased.

"I'm not going to be manish on our first date," he said, a playful gleam in his eyes. "But cute isn't the word I would use to describe you."

"You holding back? I don't believe it," she teased further. "All the stuff you talk at the gym."

"That's purely motivation, baby," he said, placing his hand on her lower back. "Gotta keep your heartbeat up."

Nicole sucked her teeth and tried to push him away. He chuckled before closing the door to her car. It was then that Nicole finally looked up at the building they were standing in front of.

"What is this place?" Nicole asked, not being able to tell by the outside of the building. She looked over at Rashaad as he smiled.

"A smash room."

"What?" Nicole asked, frowning. "Like a hotel?"

Rashaad frowned in confusion before he realized what she meant. "You wild for that," he laughed. Nicole didn't laugh, still trying to figure out where they were. "It's a room where they have a lot of random appliances and other things. They give you a bat and let you loose."

Her eyes grew wide. "Like I get to break stuff?"

"Smash," he said, smiling. Nicole laughed at his excitement.

"You've done this before? What's the point?"

"No, I haven't but I've been wanting to," he admitted. "It's basically a form of therapy. Haven't you ever wanted to break something or punch someone?" Nicole nodded. "Well, now you can legally."

Nicole giggled before nodding. "Okay, let's do it."

"That's my girl!" he said, opening the door. Nicole blushed at his indirect affirmation. She wasn't sure why, but him saying that felt good to her. It almost melted her apprehension about what was going on.

"Hi!" the woman behind the desk greeted them. Nicole politely smiled as Rashaad stepped beside her.

"I have a 6:30 reservation," he said. The woman looked at the computer and smiled.

"Baptiste?" she asked. He nodded. "Great. We just need you to sign these waivers and then we'll give you a rundown of how it works."

"Waivers?" Nicole asked. He chuckled before grabbing her hand and pulling her towards him, closer to the desk so she could see.

"Just a liability precaution," the woman said. "We haven't had any issues since we've been open."

"And how long is that?"

"Woman, chill..." Rashaad said, handing her the pen. "I wouldn't take you anywhere I felt would harm you."

Nicole looked into his eyes and relaxed. This was what she had been afraid of before. Even when they only talked online, Nicole knew he gave off the masculine energy she craved in her life. She was scared that it wasn't real, but his eyes were genuine and she felt safe with him. It made her want to relax... and she couldn't really afford to do that.

Despite her reservation, she nodded and signed the paper. As the woman gave them precautions to follow, someone else came and gave them protective covering. They had a jumpsuit, goggles and gloves.

"This is excessive," Nicole whispered. Rashaad chuckled as he fastened her glove around her wrist. He leaned in and kissed her forehead before patting her arm. "You got it. You want the bat or the crow bar?"

"The bat."

"Would you two like a custom playlist?" Nicole's eyes widened as Rashaad clapped.

"Absolutely," he said, pulling his phone out of his back pocket. "Hook me up."

Nicole giggled at his excitement. She waited to hear what he played and laughed when Meek Mill came through the speakers.

"You ready to get some aggression out?"

"You saying I'm an angry black woman?" Nicole asked.

"I'm saying you got some shit to release and I want to see it," he said, not taking the bait. Nicole looked around the room and smiled.

"You right."

The woman laughed before telling them she would start their clock as soon as she closed the door behind her. When the buzzer went off, Nicole hit a busted printer first.

"I know you can do better than that," Rashaad said, swinging at a glass vase on the other side of the room. Nicole screamed a little when it busted everywhere. "Picture what's bothering you and let that shit out."

Nicole looked around the room and saw an old flat screen television. She envisioned Julian's face and almost cringed a little. She didn't want to be a bitter baby momma, but she never planned to be one in the first place.

She tapped the screen to see how thick it was and smirked when it cracked under the pressure of the bat. She inhaled as she swung that bat back with all her might and grunted when it hit the screen again. She watched the television bend in half so she swung again and again until it finally broke.

"That's what I'm talking about!" Rashaad yelled somewhere in the room. The sound of his crowbar hitting random items almost drowning out his voice. Nicole's adrenaline pumped as she kicked over the television and rummaged to find something else to break. Her rage soon turned to her own self-doubts. Would she be able to provide for Sylar? Would she get her happily ever after? Would her child be happy? Would she continue the generational curse of broken families? Before she knew it, she was out of breath and their time was up.

Rashaad noticed she was quiet while taking off their protective gear. She struggled a little with the goggles and began to get frustrated. He gently pushed her hands down and pulled the string to loosen them.

"You good?" he asked. Nicole looked up into his eyes and her shoulders relaxed.

"I am actually," she said. Rashaad wasn't convinced. "I promise," she giggled.

"You ready to eat?" he asked.

"Yes," she said, happy that wasn't the end of their date.

Italian food was one of Nicole's favorites. She was sure she had mentioned it when she first chatted with him on the app, but neither of them mentioned it as they sat down to enjoy their food. Nicole realized there were some things she didn't know, so she decided to grill him a little.

"What do you do for real?" she asked. "I don't think we ever talked about it."

"I'm in construction."

Nicole eyed him. "Like...legally?"

"What do you think this is, the Sopranos or something?" he laughed. "Yes legally."

"My bad," she said, smiling. "So you build houses and stuff?"

"More like the inside of it. My trade is carpentry."

He can build me a house, was all Nicole thought, giggling to herself. "Was that what you wanted to do?"

He shook his head. "I want my own business. I didn't have a specific plan though. I found a trade I was good at that pays me well. I just don't work for myself yet."

She nodded. "Running a business ain't easy."

"You got a plan for all your degrees, miss thing?" he asked. Nicole smiled, touched that he remembered that from their dating app conversations.

"Well, you remember I just got in the door with this rental car company working from home? Hopefully I can get into their HR department when something opens up."

"Starting where you are is a good idea though," he said. "That'll get them used to you until your opportunity comes…"

"Why'd you ask me out?" Nicole blurted out. "What I did to you was…"

"Childish," he said after she seemed to stumble on the right word. "Petty. Cowardly. Disrespectful."

Nicole scrunched her nose to fight back tears of embarrassment. "All of that. You acting like that didn't happen is crazy. Like what is this about? Are you just trying to get some? Got a revenge plot? What?"

Rashaad looked at her and smirked. "You done?"

Nicole frowned and huffed a little. "Don't do that."

"You asking questions so let me answer." Nicole bit her bottom lip but nodded. "I'm not on none of that. I just…I vibed with you. Yeah, I was pissed you ghosted me, but I figured there was a reason."

Nicole cleared her throat. "…I um…just found out I was pregnant then. It had been months since I stopped dealing with her father and I really just wanted to talk to someone. I know that sounds cr…"

"It doesn't," he cut her off. "I get it."

Nicole smiled a little. "Yeah, well I didn't expect us to hit it off the way we did and I panicked the more you wanted to see me."

"You had me feeling like a simp," he said, shaking his head.

"I'm so sorry," she said, reaching for his hand. "I wanted to see you bad. I was just…embarrassed to even be trying to date while pregnant."

"You completely done with him?" he asked. Nicole nodded without hesitation.

"We weren't even together for real. Strictly co-parenting now."

"Nothing extra?" he asked. Nicole shook her head. "You dating anyone else?" She shook her head again.

"Should I be?" she teased.

"You can do whatever you want until I make you my woman," he said, licking his lips. "Then you're off limits. To everybody."

His tone sent a tingle down Nicole's spine. She exhaled a little before picking up her glass of wine. "Well, now that I've officially apologized and if you aren't on some revenge plot type of thing...I'm excited to officially date you." They both smiled. "If that's what we're doing."

"Oh that's what we're doing," he said, raising his glass to toast. "You can bet that."

Nicole was on a high the next few days. She couldn't believe how well their first official date went. Apparently he thought so, too, because he took her out again on her next mommy night off.

Nicole requested dinner and a movie and Rashaad made it happen. She wasn't excited about the Marvel movie he picked, but that was their deal. He picked the movie and she picked the restaurant. Their table had been cleared and the bill had been paid, yet Nicole and Rashaad hadn't made a move to leave.

"What's something you've wanted to do but never told anyone?" he asked, pushing the pads of his finger into each of her nails. Nicole smiled at the innocent touch.

"In regards to what?"

"Dating," he said. "You said you were all about doing what you want these days, right?" he asked. Nicole nodded. "So what is it?"

She bit her lip as her nose scrunched up. "I don't want to tell you."

"Why?" he chuckled.

"It's corny."

Nicole felt her skin get hot as his eyes glazed over everything that was visible to him above the table. "Nothing about you is corny."

His tone lowered just a little. Nicole felt it in the pit of her stomach. "You're just saying that."

"When have I ever just said some shit?" he asked with a blank stare. Nicole had to admit to that. Even in the short period of time she'd known him, Rashaad spoke his mind about any and everything.

She sighed. "I want to make out."

Rashaad eyed her for a moment before licking his bottom lip. "That's it?"

Nicole nodded. "That's exactly it. It's been so long since a man just kissed me just for the sake of kissing me. No expectations of sex. Just a very intimate, sensual, take my breath away make out session."

"...Um."

The silence made Nicole a little uncomfortable. If it wasn't for the lust dancing in Rashaad's eyes, she would have thought he wasn't feeling her answer. She waited a few minutes to clear her throat.

"What about you?"

"I want a woman to let me lead."

She rolled her eyes. "Oh brother."

"Hear me out," he said, holding his hands up and laughing. "Watching a woman operate in her safe space makes me feel like a man. Like I allowed her to relax and be taken care of. She lets me lead because she's soft with me...she knows she can be."

"That's what the podcast men are saying."

"I'm different, baby."

"How so?"

"I can prove I'm worth it."

The fact that Nicole believed him scared her half to death.

Although they stayed out way later than Nicole was prepared for, when he pulled up in front of her place she didn't want the night to end.

"Thank you for making mommy's day off so enjoyable."

He chuckled as he turned the car off. "It was my pleasure."

"Can we do this again?" she asked. Rashaad raised his eyebrow.

"As long as you don't ghost me again."

Nicole rolled her eyes as he laughed. "You gonna let that go?" she asked while looking down to unbuckle her seatbelt. She gasped when she looked up and his face was only a few inches from hers. She inhaled as he pushed at her nose with his, making her look up into his eyes.

"I might," he said against her lips before wrapping his around her bottom lip. Nicole leaned against the middle console as he slowly applied more pressure to the kiss. She hummed when his left hand came around the side of her neck, his thumb rubbing her jawline as the other fingers pressed into her skin. The groan that came from his throat made her weak and she was thankful to be seated at that moment. Nicole's body relaxed as the kiss deepened, allowing him access inside, Rashaad skillfully wrapped his tongue around hers.

"I appreciate you spending time with me," he said, in between kisses. Nicole's breathing picked up as she nodded, wanting him to stop talking and keep kissing her. She sucked his bottom lip and accidently bit it, hard. When he pulled away with wide eyes her face felt hot.

"I'm sorry," she said, rubbing it with her thumb. He kissed her finger before placing her hand on his chest. Nicole closed her eyes as he mimicked her, but nibbled on her lip instead of biting it. He licked around her bottom lip before kissing her harder. She wasn't sure how much time had passed before they came up for air.

Rashaad sighed. "Let me walk you..."

Nicole cut him off by crawling over the console and sitting in his lap. She put both hands on either side of his neck before kissing him again with her tongue leading the way. Rashaad groaned as he gripped her hips, pulling her closer. Her heart wanted to explode as she realized what he had done.

"Thank you for listening to me," she said, giving him quick peaks, deciding she loved his lips.

"I'ma do that as long as you talking to me," he said. Nicole blushed. "Did it meet your expectations?" She kissed him hard before pulling back to look at him. "Good." They both laughed. "Come on. Let's get you in the house."

chapter ten

Although Nicole still counted time in weeks, the days with Rashaad in her life were filled with so much joy. He was so intentional with Nicole and although it scared her, she wasn't backing down from his affection.

She noticed that he was very affectionate, but they still hadn't crossed the line of intimacy. It wasn't as if she didn't try, she'd tried on several occasions. She's been subtle with her advances and he dodged them every time.

But tonight was her Sylar-free night and Nicole planned to show him her appreciation. She invited him over for a home cooked meal and to spend the night. Since he accepted, that meant he was finally ready to go all the way.

Instead of him coming to the house, Nicole got up early to get Sylar ready and dropped her off at Julian's before she went to pamper herself. It had been a while since she had a mani pedi and today seemed like the perfect excuse. All of her other upkeep had been done prior to today; she decided not to bother with her hair. Rashaad liked it when it was free and a little frizzy.

When she got home, Nicole took a nap before prepping her food. However, her doorbell ringing earlier than expected interrupted her nap.

"Baby," she squealed, waiting for him to put his bag down before jumping into his arms. "What are you doing here so early?"

He kissed her forehead before kissing her lips. "Hey gorgeous."

Nicole blushed, getting comfortable in his embrace. He walked her backwards far enough to close and lock her front door.

"Hi," she said, holding her head back and pushing her lips out. He chuckled as he kissed her again.

"I'm early because I can be," he teased, pinching her hip. Nicole sucked her teeth before removing herself from his embrace and grabbing his bag.

"I didn't start cooking yet," she said, walking to take his bag to her bedroom. He waited until she was back to pull her on the couch.

"Just cool it with me, baby," he said, kissing her cheek.

Nicole was already annoyed with the amount of blushing he caused. "My cheeks hurt already."

He laughed before adjusting their position to get more comfortable.

"What did you do all day?" He pulled at her fingers. "Your nails look good. Let me see your toes."

She laughed harder. "How do you know I got them done?"

Rashaad grinned while ignoring her question, she continued to laugh as he playfully pushed her back against the couch far enough that he could pull her feet into his lap. Nicole held her breath as he pushed his thumb into the arch of her foot.

"They look good," he said. "My favorite color." He looked up at her to see if she'd done that on purpose. The grin on her face confirmed it. "What are you up to?" He kissed her ankle.

Nicole shook her head. "You want to watch our show for a little while before I cook?" Rashaad nodded so she hopped up, and grabbed the remote from her coffee table.

They cuddled on the couch as Nicole traveled to Netflix to pull up Dark. It was something she would have never watched on her own, but she loved watching it with him. Apparently he watched it before but didn't want to tell her. Now that she figured it out, she asked questions the whole show. He ignored her and usually just kissed her shoulder or cheek and told her to keep watching.

"You smell good, baby," he said, burying his face into her neck.

"Thank you."

"You're welcome." He kissed her between each word.

Nicole wasn't sure how her heart hadn't burst open just yet. She never believed in love languages until he came along. The way he affirmed her with words and actions made her feel like she was floating. She thought it would stop after the first few weeks but here she was…floating higher.

She couldn't explain it, but his intentions matching his words and his actions did something to her. Nicole felt safe with him, emotionally and physically. She never had that in her adult life.

Feeling herself get emotional, she sighed. "Let me get dinner started. Don't watch the next one without me."

He nodded while turning Netflix off. She was sure she would hear sports soon. She decided on a simple dinner, cube steak with gravy, mashed potatoes, and broccoli. She was seasoning the steak when he strolled into the kitchen and sat across from her on an island stool. She waited a few minutes to see if he would say anything but he didn't.

"You need something?" she asked, not looking up from her prep work.

"Yeah...for you to be mine."

Her hand movement slowed as she processed his words. "Yours as in..."

"My woman," he confirmed. "Officially mine anyway." Nicole exhaled as she sat the seasoning down. She looked up at him and nodded but he shook his head. "Verbal consent, love."

"I'm okay with that," she said before clearing her throat and going back to her task at hand. She felt her skin get hot the more he stayed quiet. "Anything else?" she teased, trying to shake off her emotions.

"Look at me, Nicole." Rashaad waited until he had her attention. "Tell me why that made you emotional, baby."

"It didn't," she lied.

He could tell. "Try again."

Nicole dropped her hands on the counter. "It's stupid. It shouldn't have made me emotional. I'm okay."

He was up and around the counter before she could even blink. She groaned as he grabbed both her hands and turned her to face him. Lifting her chin up, he gave her the sweetest kiss she ever had in her life. If that didn't make her cry, what he said next did.

"Baby, I promise you nothing you ever feel for me will be stupid. It might make you feel happy or horny...but never stupid. You know me well enough by now to know that I'm about all of you. You can be real with me. I won't make you feel stupid for trusting me or feeling good about being mine. Baby, that makes me feel like that nigga to know you feel that way." Nicole giggled. "I feel the same way."

"Yeah?" she asked, the softness in her voice matching his. He nodded before kissing her forehead.

"I don't know if you know or not, but women out here are wild, too," he said. Nicole nodded in agreement. "Most of them ain't checking for an honest, hard working man like myself. You look at me like I'm interesting as hell and I know I'm not." He laughed. "I'm boring, baby."

Nicole rolled her eyes and laughed. "Well, I like you cause I'm boring, too…aight?" They both laughed at her movie reference.

"Well, we're gonna be a boring ass, fine ass couple together… aight?"

She kissed him hard. Not wanting to say anything else that would make her sound naive or unaccustomed to this princess treatment, showing him all she felt in that moment.

Rashaad stayed in the kitchen and kept Nicole company while she finished cooking. He even fixed her sink that had been leaking for the last couple of weeks. He asked if anything else needed to be fixed and although Nicole was renting, she happily gave him a list of things that her landlord hadn't gotten to.

They enjoyed dinner and settled in for the night and Nicole had to admit to feeling a little less anxious about their relationship as the night went on. They fit so well. It was natural and organic and Nicole didn't feel like she was overcompensating for anything.

After a little back and forth, Nicole agreed to let him clean up the kitchen while she took a shower. She made sure to use her in-shower moisturizer so her skin would be extra soft. Not wanting to seem too obvious, but also wanting to entice him, Nicole put on a blue rib knit lounge set that was a pair of shorts and a camisole top. She kept her locs down but made sure her bonnet was on the nightstand. He was still in the living room watching sports center when she got out.

"Hey," she said, peeking her head around the corner of her open bedroom door.

"You left some hot water?" he teased, turning the television off as he got up. Nicole nodded as she watched him walk closer to her. He gave her three quick kisses before grabbing the back of her neck to kiss her deeper. "You gonna stay up for me?" he asked against her lips.

"Yes."

He looked down at her while biting his bottom lip. "Good."

Nicole moved aside to let him into the bedroom. Her bathroom was connected, so she busied herself with removing the pillows on her bed as he grabbed a few things out of his bag and headed into the bathroom. Her nerves got the best of her so she called Raina when she heard the shower cut on.

"Y'all done already? Dang, that sucks."

"Haven't even started yet." Raina laughed. "Shut up and tell me why I'm nervous."

"Hell if I know. I need to walk you through it?"

"I wasn't even nervous until he asked me to officially be his woman."

"Well, that's ass backwards. That should make you more comfortable."

"I don't want him to regret his decision..."

"Nicole, don't make me slap you. That man has proven himself. Now he is committed to you. Be a big girl and put him to sleep."

Nicole giggled. "Shut up. I'm getting off the phone with you."

"Remember that trick I told you about!"

"Bye!"

Nicole took a deep breath before putting her phone on the charger and getting herself together. She wondered if she should light a candle but decided against it. She did turn Youtube on her television and played her R&B playlist.

"Your water pressure slaps," he said, coming back into the room. Nicole giggled before she noticed he was still in his towel.

"I'm glad you like it," she said as he closed the gap between them. Nicole groaned as he gripped the back of her neck to bring her lips to his.

"You been so good to me today, baby," he said. Nicole whimpered against his lips before wrapping her arms around his waist. "Looking fine and feeding me." He kissed her neck. "Officially becoming mine...Can I take care of you now?"

"Yes," she said, leaning back to look into his eyes. She wanted to be clear that she wanted everything he had to offer. Rashaad rubbed her chin with his thumb before pecking her lips a few times.

"You sure?" Nicole nodded and quickly gasped as Rashaad pushed his hands under her camisole and kneaded both of her breasts. "Say you're sure."

"I'm sure, baby."

"Good girl."

Nicole grinned as her vision became hazy. Rashaad stepped forward a few times until Nicole's thighs hit the side of the bed. While slowly kissing her, he cuffed the back of her knees so her butt hit the bed. He pulled up to lay her back with her knees bent. She watched him bite his bottom lip while sliding her shorts off.

"Take that shirt off." She did as he demanded. He told her not to move as he let her leg go and went over to his bag. Nicole rested her feet on the bed before watching him pull a box of condoms out. She wondered how many he planned to use. She sighed when he came back and kissed her calf while raising her legs completely in the air. She almost felt helpless just laying there so she tried to sit up. Rashaad pushed her back down before he got on his knees and pushed her legs into the butterfly position.

"Where you going?"

"Baby," she whined.

"What?" He sucked on her inner thigh while smacking the outside of it. "I don't need your help right now." With her legs still in a butterfly position, he pushed both of his thumbs into the arch of her feet as he gently nipped at her thighs, making her jump each time. Nicole couldn't form the words to beg him to stop teasing her, so she just laid there and took it.

Nicole sighed as he finally slid his tongue across her lower lips. She could feel her toes tingle from the pressure his thumbs applied. Rashaad groaned as he French kissed his new friend, releasing her legs so he could push his face deeper.

"Oh, just like that baby," Nicole encouraged, rubbing his locs with her left hand. He looked up at her and smirked as he pushed two fingers inside.

"I told you I didn't need your help, didn't I?"

Nicole's head fell back as she leaned up on her elbows. "I'm sorry."

"Not yet," he said, standing up tall as his towel dropped. "But you will be."

After a great evening, Nicole woke up very relaxed. Having a man, her man, lying next to her felt good. She shifted to get a better look at him and giggled to see his mouth slightly open. She said her morning prayer, making sure to include Rashaad before quietly sliding out of bed. Nicole took a shower and blushed while cleaning her body. She hated to compare the two, but he was different from Julian in many ways.

Having Rashaad made Nicole realize just how much of a fool she had been in the past. Sure, Julian wasn't disrespectful or even mean to her, but he wasn't caring. He didn't spend the night. He didn't show affection the way Rashaad did. He didn't take his time with her. Nicole sighed as she decided to go cook breakfast.

It was almost as if another person popped into her head. The voice wasn't unfamiliar, but it was one that Nicole thought she dealt with months ago.

"Look at you, cooking for this man and being all giddy just because he asked you to be his woman. He hasn't proven himself yet."

Nicole signed as she shook her head, looking around the kitchen for a distraction from her intrusive thoughts. She pulled her phone out of the pocket of her robe and turned her Apple Music on shuffle. Jaheim's smooth voice flowed through, putting a smile on her phone. She put her phone on the counter and continued to make breakfast.

Of course Rashaad had proven himself...thus far. Not only did he look over the fact that she ghosted him after starting an emotional relationship with him while pregnant with another man's baby, but he'd been intentional while they dated and didn't take too long to make her his woman.

But she didn't know all of his intentions. Did he want marriage? Would he want a child of his own? Would he want them to live together before marriage? Would he expect her to pay bills? Nicole sighed, feeling a headache coming on as these questions bombarded her euphoric feelings from the night before.

"I need a damn therapist," she mumbled. "This is crazy."

"You in here talking to yourself?"

Nicole jumped a little as Rashaad's warm hands wrapped around her waist. She smirked as he kissed her neck but quickly frowned at him rubbing her belly.

"Don't rub my fat like that," she said, trying to pry his hands off of her. He groaned into her neck before gripping her tighter.

"I did last night," he said. Nicole's mouth closed. "And I'll do what I want."

"So you say," she mumbled, trying to find some resolve to fight back.

"I do say," he demanded, biting her neck. Nicole's body relaxed into his embrace but her insides were on fire, just that quick.

"Can I finish your breakfast?" she whispered as he slowly swayed them side to side to whatever was playing. Nicole couldn't even hear it at this point. The hum in his throat was drowning out all of her senses. He kept rubbing her belly, but his kisses slowed down and eventually turned into licks. When

Nicole felt him tug on the knot of her robe, she reached up and turned the stove off.

A few days after they became official, Nicole was ignoring Rashaad's calls.
And she was completely the problem.

The day after, she'd gotten a flower delivery with the sweetest note she'd ever read.

I appreciate you trusting me with your heart and your body.

I promise to take care of it like you deserve.

He didn't even have to say much but those two sentences spoke to every fear she had about being with that man. He just knew what to say and that scared the hell out of her. Nicole felt stupid. She often wondered what was wrong with women that she saw treat a good man bad because she wasn't used to it. She just knew once she got one that didn't play about her she wouldn't play about him. Yet here she was in her clown suit.

"I ought to drop kick you," Raina said from her seat on the couch in her living room. Nicole shook her head as she tapped the hanging toy on the play mat that Raina bought for Sylar. She was reaching for things now and that made Nicole want to cry. "Answer the phone for that man."

"I think I should break up with him and try therapy first."

"You sound dumb as hell."

Nicole gasped before laughing in shock. "Dang cousin, tell me how you really feel?"

"For months I kept shit cute with you because you claim I try to run your life, but you were slower than molasses when you were dealing with Julian. This man has uno reversed all that bad situationship karma and decided to claim your ass after you ghosted him and you think breaking up with him is the answer? I didn't raise you right at all."

"Raina, he's too good to be true!" Nicole whined. "You literally just mentioned how I ghosted him. You think he's not remembering that?"

"Didn't he say he let it go?"

Nicole shrugged. "I don't believe it." Raina rubbed her forehead before sitting back on the couch and grabbing the remote. Nicole raised her eyebrow as she began to flip through channels. "I have a right to be cautious."

"You spelled stupid wrong."

Nicole gasped. "You're rude as hell."

"I'm done talking to you about it," Raina shrugged. "Fumble that man again if you want to."

Nicole was shocked to see Rashaad's car next to her usual spot when she pulled up in front of her apartment. She swallowed the lump in her throat once she saw his stone facial expression as he got out of the car. She tried to walk around to get Sylar out the backseat, but he stopped her, pushing her up against the closed passenger side door. Nicole felt her skin heat under his gaze as he took her purse and put it on the hood of the car.

Rashaad tilted his head back to move his locs from his face but they fell right back into place as he looked down at her. He slid both his hands up her neck using his thumbs to rub her jawline. Nicole's breathing increased as she waited impatiently for him to say something. Her mouth dropped open when he finally spoke.

"I apologize."

Nicole cleared her throat before she whispered. "For what?"

"I must have given you the impression that I was a lame ass nigga who you could duck and dodge when you wanted to. That's my fault."

Nicole whimpered when he went to back away from her a little, but hadn't let her go. She gripped his shirt with both hands to keep him in her space.

"I don't think that," she said as tears pooled in her eyes. "I don't. I'm sorry...I."

"You do," he insisted. "I let you pull that shit once so you think it's cool. Be a big girl and tell me you don't want to be with me."

Nicole violently shook her head. "That's not it." She tried to kiss him but he frowned and moved out of her reach. She mentally kicked herself for ignoring him. Her body was clearly mad at her as well. She glanced to see if Sylar had woken up in the car and sighed when he adjusted her chin to make her look at him.

"Tell me I'm wasting my time."

"I want to be with you," she managed. "I don't want to hurt you," she made sure to say. "You just feel too good to be true."

She whispered that last part, but the frown on his face assured Nicole that he heard her. He dropped his hands from her neck and this time she did let him go, seeing his frustration.

"I'm not going to keep having this conversation with you, Nicole. I'm here because I want to be." She just watched him. "If you were in my position you'd feel like shit right?" She finally nodded. "So why you doing it to me?"

"I'm not doing it intentionally."

"It feels like it," he said. "It really fucking feels like it."

In that moment, Nicole felt horrible. She knew exactly how it would feel because she'd been in his position not too long ago. She was so worried about him hurting her that she was hurting him. She felt him slipping away and that made the tears fall. She tried to wipe them before he saw but it was too late.

"I don't want to make you cry, but.."

She shook her head. "You didn't. I did. You're right." She reached for him and although he hesitated, Rashaad made his way back into her space.

"I don't want to have to question how you move, mama," he said, finally hugging her. "Tighten up."

She nodded. "Can you come inside?" she asked, not wanting to talk outside anymore.

Rashaad looked at her for a minute before shaking his head. Nicole frowned but he opened the back door and got Sylar out before handing her to Nicole.

"I need to think," he said. Nicole's heartbroke a little but she understood. He made sure they got in safely before leaving.

chapter eleven

She assumed after her apology that things would go back to normal, but Rashaad hadn't been back to her place since that night a week ago. He was answering her calls, but anytime she tried to initiate quality time, he declined it. Nicole knew that he was trying to prove a point, but how could she prove hers if he wouldn't let her?

Today she had reached her breaking point and had come up with a plan to get back into her man's good graces. It took her some time to come up with a plan because she couldn't tell Raina what was going on and she was usually the mastermind. Nicole just wasn't in the mood to hear "I told you so."

It was Saturday morning so Nicole knew that Rashaad would be at the gym. After feeding and bathing Sylar, she put on one of the few matching workout sets she owned and headed to Julian's. Once she was in his parking lot, she called his phone.

"You were serious about coming this early?" he groaned.

"Yes, she went back to sleep and she's already had her morning bottle."

"Where do you have to be this early?"

"Mind your business and come get your daughter," she said, hanging up by pressing the End button on her console. A few minutes later, Julian's door opened. She watched him run both his hands down his face as he looked to see where she was parked. Nicole hit the unlock button before she turned to make sure Sylar was still sleeping. A few moments later, Julian opened the back door. He looked over the carseat at Nicole and frowned.

"You woke me up this early to go to the gym?" he asked. Nicole unclicked the seatbelt and rolled her eyes.

"Bye baby daddy."

Julian's nose flared before he took Sylar's carseat out of the base. Nicole smirked, knowing that he hated to be called that. He closed the door without another word. She waited until they were inside before she reversed out of the spot and headed to the gym.

Seeing Rashaad's truck made her relieved and anxious at the same time. Pulling her locs back into a ponytail, she took a moment to think of what she'd say before getting out of the car.

Obviously, her apology hadn't been enough for things to go back to normal, but Nicole realized that was the problem. She'd finally gotten what she wanted; a man...a good man that was willing to commit to her. She had to put her apprehension and trust issues aside, especially since Rashaad hadn't done anything to deserve them.

Nicole quickly made her way to the locker room, secured her bag and then walked back out into the main room of the gym. She looked around for a moment before she saw him on a Smith machine. Taking a deep breath, she walked over and stood behind him so that he could see her. He was about to chest press the bar. Rashaad looked her up and down before going back to his seat. Nicole bit her lip, waiting for him to speak.

"What are you doing here so early?" he asked.

"Wanted to work out with you," she said, softly. He finished his set before sitting up, his elbows on his knees.

"You sure?" he asked, looking up at her with a smirk. Nicole's heart dropped knowing what she just signed up for but there was no backing down now. She nodded. "You warm up yet?" She shook her head. "Get to it."

Nicole waited until she turned towards the elliptical to roll her eyes. He was not going to make this easy for her at all. She watched him talk to a few guys and joke around while she did her ten minutes on the elliptical. She thought he wasn't paying attention to her until she had about ten seconds left and he turned to watch her. She quickly looked down at the machine before finishing the time and hopping off. His loud clap caused her to jump a little from across the room.

"Let's go, baby!" he said, looking at her. "Time to work!"

Nicole groaned as a few of his friends chuckled before he moved the bench out of the way as she walked over. She was grateful that he moved to take some of the weight off, but when he stopped and there was still more than she was used to she wanted to cry.

"Come on and do these squats."

"It's leg day?" she asked. He nodded before gently pushing on her lower back to move her in position. She braced herself and realized it wasn't that bad once she did one rep.

"Don't smile now," he said. "You're going up 5 pounds every set."

"You don't have to do all this," she groaned.

"You wanted to work out with me right?" he asked, looking at her through the mirror with a smirk. Nicole huffed but continued her set.

20 minutes later and Nicole's legs felt like noodles. After the squats, they did RDLs and sumo squats. When they got to the pulses, she wanted to throw up. She had to admit that it was nice working out with him. It reminded her of the fantasy she had when they first ran back into each other. He definitely showed her things she wouldn't have done on her own, but now she was over it. He was dragging it.

When her watch beeped that she had reached her move goal for the day, she flopped down on the ground. "You win."

"Win what? You got one more."

"No, I don't," she whined. Rashaad laughed before pulling her up. She groaned but when he wrapped his arms around her and kissed her forehead, she whimpered.

"Stop whining. You did good, baby."

"You done being mad at me?" she asked, looking up at him and pulling on one of his locs.

"I wasn't mad anymore after you apologized," he said, letting her go but grabbing her hand. "Let's go stretch."

Nicole watched his shoulder flex as he walked in front of her and sighed. "Can we stretch at home?"

Rashaad turned and looked at her over his shoulder before laughing. "Stop it."

Nicole smirked after seeing him blush. "You're so fine and handsome."

Rashaad shook his head as he continued to lead her to the stretching area. He wiped down two mats before putting them side by side near the wall. She waited for his instruction before they began to stretch. They settled into a comfortable silence until he leaned over and bit her shoulder.

"I missed you," he said. Nicole felt her body relax even though she was already feeling the workout.

"I missed you more."

"You with me for real now?" he asked, looking directly in her eyes. Nicole looked back and nodded without hesitation. He looked at her for a moment before he ran his thumb over her jaw. "Good."

chapter twelve

"She's driving me crazy today," Nicole admitted. "Like she wants to see how long it'll take me to crack. She's a terrorist."

Marie laughed. "Don't talk about my sweet baby like that."

"Well, your sweet baby will be right at your doorstep tonight if she doesn't cool it," Nicole teased.

"You can bring her. I'm not doing anything tonight."

Nicole's eyes widened. "Auntie, I was just playing. We just had a long day..."

"Which means you can use a break. I'm sure you want to spend time with that man of yours and I've been told you still won't let him meet baby girl."

Nicole rolled her eyes at Raina telling all her business. She decided not to mention it with the opportunity at hand. "Really?"

"Um hum. Pack her up. She can go to church with me in the morning." Nicole wanted to cry. "If you make it that long anyway."

She giggled. "I can. I can run some errands in the morning..."

"Aht!" Marie said. "I ain't keeping her if you gonna do all that. I said relax."

"Yes, ma'am."

"See you in a few."

Nicole would have felt bad with how fast she packed Sylar's bag if she wasn't confident that her aunt loved her baby almost as much as she did. Nicole's support system was A1, but she still tried not to put too much responsibility on them when it came to Sylar. However, spending the night with Rashaad didn't sound like the worst idea.

It had been weeks since their first fight and although Nicole still had a war within herself, Rashaad had been a man of his word. Their schedule didn't always align, but he did his best to accommodate her since she hadn't let him meet Sylar yet. She wasn't even sure why, but most of her reservations were gone. He had come close that night she was sleeping in the car, but that didn't count.

She waited until she got back to her empty home to call him and see if he wanted to spend the night and he accepted.

"You cooking?" he asked.

"I would baby, but I'm a little tired," she admitted. "You mind picking something up? Unless you just really want me to cook. I could do..."

"What you want to eat?" he asked. Nicole smiled.

"Shrimp fried rice?"

"You such a cheap date," he teased. Nicole gasped as he laughed.

"Just for that you gotta take me to the steak house this weekend."

"Not a problem, mama," he said. Nicole closed her eyes, relishing in his voice. His tone and how he easily agreed to things with her made her feel so wanted. "Anything else?"

Just you..... "Nope."

After mindless television and dinner, Nicole took a quick shower and tried to busy herself while Rashaad did the same. She was tired and wanted nothing more than to curl up next to him and go to sleep, but she didn't want to disappoint him if he was in the mood for sex. He'd been flirty and playful all night so Nicole was sure that was where his mind was.

She was sitting up against the headboard of her bed when he walked into the room. She put her phone down when he leaned over and kissed her forehead. She watched as he leaned back and looked at her for a moment before motioning for her to sit up. When there was enough space, he slid behind her, replacing his back with hers and wrapping her up in his arms.

"Tell me what you need, mama," Rashaad said, pushing his full lips into the side of Nicole's neck. She let out a breathless moan as her whole body relaxed.

"I love when you call me that," she admitted. The chuckle he released against her skin let her know he knew exactly what his words and voice did to her.

"Why?"

"I don't know," she whined. The sting against her thigh made her swallow the whine as soon as it came out.

"You know I don't like the whining," he said, wrapping his free hand around her neck. "Use your words."

Nicole's head felt so heavy she let it fall back against his chest. Putting her full weight on him, Rashaad's body was strong, not budging at all or distracting him from his task at hand.

"I can't think."

"You heard what I said."

Nicole bit her lip to keep from whining again. "It makes my whole body tingle. I feel like I'm going to explode."

"Um," he said, licking her neck. "Good girl." Nicole turned to straddle his waist and kissed him hard. She pushed her hands into the back of the headboard behind him before wrapping them around his neck. Rashaad gripped her hips to drive her even closer. "Tell me what else I want to hear."

"I'm yours," she said without hesitation. This caused him to kiss her just as hard.

"What else?" he asked in a softer tone, pushing the straps of her nightgown down.

"I trust you," she whispered, moaning as he kissed her shoulder.

"What else?"

They loved each other. There wasn't any doubt about it at this point. Nicole knew he was waiting for her to say it and she was trying her hardest not to before him. It had been frustrating at first, but now that she was confident based on his actions it felt like a game…almost like foreplay.

"What else you need from me, baby?" she asked, sucking his bottom lip. She looked up into his eyes while doing it to see him already staring down into hers. A low groan escaped his throat as she began to rotate her hips against him. "Hum?"

"For you to go to sleep."

Nicole's movements stopped as she opened her eyes and looked at him. He seemed unbothered by his comment as he kept kissing along her collarbone.

"Right now?" she asked. He nodded.

"You're tired." It wasn't a question.

"Yea, but…"

Rashaad shifted them to where they were laying down before pulling the comforter over their body. Nicole was still on top of him, but closed her legs so that his were on the outside.

"Then go to sleep, mama," he said, kissing her forehead. "I ain't going nowhere."

If she wasn't sure before, she definitely loved this man. With his heartbeat under her and his warm hands rubbing her back, Nicole was asleep before she knew it.

Her body jerked her awake to a dark room and an immense amount of pressure between her legs. She groaned as she blinked a few times, trying to gather herself but the pressure gained momentum by the second. She gasped as she realized what was going on and her right hand immediately pushed against the top of his head.

"Baby," she groaned, pulling her legs further apart. Rashaad only went harder now that she was awake.

"Did you sleep good, mama?" he asked. Nicole nodded incessantly.

"Yes," she drew out.

"Um," he moaned before moving to lick her thigh. "Good."

Nicole's eyes rolled as he continued his assault. Her body suddenly shook as if it realized what was going on. Rashaad chuckled as he kissed up her chest, burying his face into her neck. Nicole's body relaxed around him as he slid inside of her.

"You ever had morning sex?" he asked, biting into her neck. She shook her head, wrapping her arms around his back. "Wasn't it worth the wait?"

"Yes," she said, knowing he wouldn't be satisfied if she didn't say it verbally. He rewarded her with a deeper stroke. "You always know just what I need."

"That's my job," he growled. "I'ma always do that."

Tears threatened to fall from Nicole's face as she pushed her head into the pillow, moving both of their locs out of the way, she turned her head to kiss him. The dryness of their morning breath was quickly replaced with their passion.

"If I ever stop, you tell me."

"Stop right now," she blurted out while groaning. Rashaad chuckled.

"You really want me to stop?"

"It's too much."

"Nah it ain't," he said, going faster. "You deserve it."

Those three words were enough for Nicole to want to pass out. Instead, she felt her body explode and all of her senses wake up.

After her wake up call, the two showered together before making breakfast. Nicole knew it was too soon to think about living together but she loved having him in her space. It wasn't at all like she thought it would be. He was a little messy, but he cleaned up after himself for the most part. She could see him being around her and Sylar on lazy days, enjoying each other's company. Speaking of Sylar...

"I'm throwing Sy a half birthday party," she blurted out. Rashaad continued to lace up his sneakers.

"That's a thing?" he chuckled. Nicole sucked her teeth.

"Yes and don't judge me," she said. He shook his head before smiling at her.

"I won't, mama. When are you doing it?"

"This weekend at my aunt's house. She has the most space."

"You'll have to let me know how it goes," he said, standing up to walk over to his bag.

"I want you there," she said, biting her lip while awaiting his reaction. He was reaching down to grab the strap of his bag but stood back up and turned to her. She smiled as he questioned her with his eyes. She smiled in assurance. He walked back over to her, leaning down to her position on the bed and kissed her.

"I'll be there."

chapter thirteen

Today they were celebrating Sylar's ½ birthday. Everyone thought Nicole was doing too much, but when the day finally came everyone was excited. Although Nicole was ecstatic to be celebrating, she was nervous. Today, Rashaad would be meeting Sylar....and Julian.

Ever since they both apologized, Nicole and Rashaad were inseparable. He had truly proven to Nicole that he was committed and she believed him. He hinted at meeting Sylar a few times but hadn't pressured her and Nicole was grateful for that. She'd worry about them meeting later but she had to decorate her aunt's living room. Raina came to help. The theme was, Halfway to One. There were orange and gold steamers, balloons and tassels everywhere.

"I think we may have overdid it," Raina said. Marie snickered. "You two always do," she said. "Sylar has no hope."

"She'll be well rounded," Raina said. Nicole laughed but didn't respond. "You still nervous over there?"

Nicole shrugged. "What if she doesn't like him?"

"She's a baby...she hardly likes you."

"Be for real," Nicole rolled her eyes. "I'm her bestie."

"That's just because you feed her," Raina said. They laughed. "But no seriously. What's the worst that could happen? It's not like you're about to leave her with him or something. He's more so meeting the family."

Nicole nodded. "And that's another thing."

"Nobody cares about her daddy," Raina said, knowing what Nicole was about to say. "Didn't you invite his girl?"

Nicole nodded. She hadn't wanted to, but she did extend the invite to anyone Julian wanted to come. She only did it so he wouldn't have any ammo to point out why Rashaad was there.

"It'll all be fine," Marie said, patting both her girls on their backs. "Where is my sister?"

Nicole rolled her eyes. "You know she'll be here once all the work is done."

Nobody really talked about Nicole's relationship with her mom. Their relationship has always been strained. Nicole was closer to Marie and even lived with her and Raina as a teen. Moving out helped a little because they didn't argue as much, but Nicole still wasn't her favorite person.

Someone knocked on the door and Marie went to open it. She came back with Julian and his mom, Joyce.

"Hope you don't mind us coming early," Joyce said.

"Of course not. Sy's still sleeping but she'll need to get up and get ready soon," Nicole said. Joyce purchased the dress that Sylar would be wearing that day. "Let me show you where she is."

Joyce and Nicole went towards the back of the house where Raina's old bedroom was. "I've never been to a ½ birthday," Joyce giggled.

"Me neither," Nicole confessed. "I've just seen it online and wanted to do it."

"She deserves to be celebrated," Joyce said, making Nicole smile. "You do as well. You're doing amazing with my grandbaby."

Nicole always admired Joyce and how well she took care of her family. When she did work for Julian and Pierre, they hosted annual bbqs and other events where their parents were present. She was always pleasant to Nicole but she knew it was a shock to her that she and Julian were messing around. Joyce had never been introduced to Nicole as anything other than the assistant before Sylar came along.

"Thank you," Nicole said. "That means a lot." She opened Raina's bedroom door to see Sylar lying in the middle of the bed surrounded by pillows. She was up on her belly and looked straight at both of them when they came in. "Hey pretty girl!"

Joyce went straight to her, cooing and picking her up. Nicole giggled, loving that Sylar had so much love around her.

"You want to get her ready?" Nicole asked, already knowing Joyce would say yes. She nodded. "Everything should be in her bag and there's a bathroom right next door."

"Got it."

Nicole left them to it as she went back into the living room. "Everyone else still coming?"

Julian nodded before looking around. "Where's the cake?"

"I'm leaving to go get it now," Raina said. "It's not far."

"Thanks cousin," Nicole said, sighing as she realized everything was done. She excused herself to go make sure Rashaad was still coming. Going into her aunt's bedroom, she closed the door and Facetimed him.

Earlier when she'd talked to him, he had his locs down. Now they were pulled into a low ponytail making his entire face visible. He'd gotten a line up and his goatee looked amazing. Nicole bit her lip when he answered, forgetting to even greet him.

He chuckled. "Thank you for the compliment, mama."

Nicole blushed. "I was just checking to see if you'd be here on time?"

His right eyebrow raised. "I ever not get to you on time?"

"No," she whispered.

"I'm in the car now," he said, panning the phone so she could see the inside of his car. She smiled to see the large orange bag in his backseat. "Where's baby girl?"

"Her granny is getting her dressed."

He nodded. "You nervous?"

"Just a little."

"I'll be on my best behavior, mama."

"Here you go with this mama mess," Nicole said.

"You should have never told me what it does to you," he said, laughing. The camera shifted as he put his phone in the holder attached to his air vent. "You need anything before I get there?"

"Just you."

It was a simple gesture, but they both knew how much Nicole tried to control her emotions in the relationship they were building. Rashaad knew better than to verbally acknowledge it, but that didn't stop him from smiling. He tried to stifle it by biting his bottom lip. They fell into a comfortable silence with Nicole watching him drive until he reminded her she was hosting a party.

"Oh crap," she said, standing up as he laughed. "I'll see you when you get here."

When Nicole emerged from the room, Joyce had Sylar out and dressed and everyone was there. Raina was walking back in with the cake as Julian took Sylar from Joyce. Nicole frowned.

"Where's Tessica?"

"You invited her?" Deniece asked. Nicole looked around at everyone looking at her and she shrugged.

"I told him he could invite who he wanted," Nicole said, looking at Julian who was doing his best to ignore the conversation. "I just assumed..."

It seemed that Julian invited everyone important in his life. Even Pierre and Sage were there so it was safe for her to assume he would have extended the invitation to his woman. Nicole couldn't decipher the look Deniece gave Julian but she decided not to dwell on it. It was true she was hoping Tessica could be a buffer for introducing Rashaad to Julian. But, oh well.

The doorbell rang and Nicole instantly felt butterflies in her stomach. She excused herself from the living room and went to answer the door. Instantly lighting up at his presence, Nicole rushed into his arms.

"Baby," she said, placing both hands on his face and kissing him. "You brought me flowers? Aren't you sweet!"

"Give me another one real quick," he said, looking down at her lips. Nicole giggled. "These ain't for you." He laughed at her shocked face. Nicole sucked her teeth.

"Come on," she said, moving to let him in. After closing the door, she took the gift bag from him and rolled her eyes at the flowers. He grinned before hugging her with his free hand and kissing her forehead. Satisfied with his affection, she led him into the living room. Nicole cleared her throat to get everyone's attention.

"Hey family...this is Rashaad. Rashaad, this is everyone."

"Nice to finally meet you," Marie said, walking up first. "I'm Aunt Marie."

"Nice to meet you," he said after she hugged him. "My momma taught me never to go to a woman's house empty handed." She gasped in shock as he handed her the flowers. Nicole tried not to smile.

"Finally one with some sense," she said, excusing herself to find a vase. Rashaad gave Nicole a sly smirk.

"Whatever," she said, blushing. Raina had Sylar so they walked over there next.

"And this is the half birthday girl," Nicole said, giggling.

"Pictures don't do you justice, little mama," he said, tapping her hand that gripped Raina's shirt. Sylar just looked around, lying her head down. "You must be Raina?"

"None other," she said. "I thought you met baby girl already?"

"Not while she's awake," he said.

"Well, don't get used to her smiling at you. Those are reserved for me," she joked. They all laughed.

While Raina joked about being Sylar's favorite. Julian walked over and tried to take her. Raina frowned but allowed him to.

"Hey," Nicole said. "Babe, this is Sylar's father, Julian. Julian, this is Rashaad."

"What's up, man?" Rashaad said, nodding. Julian gave him a once over before nodding as well but not saying anything. Nicole rolled her eyes before he walked off with Sylar. Rashaad just chuckled.

"You hungry?" Nicole asked, running her thumb over his arm. He smiled down at her before kissing her forehead.

"Hook me up, mama."

Nicole took a deep breath to reel her body in. It was as if all of her anxious energy was transferred into the hyper awareness that took over when her man was around. She sighed, loving that she had a safe space to claim.

Fixing his plate as he asked about how the party was going so far, they were interrupted when Deniece walked into the kitchen.

"Excuse me, I just came for some more meatballs," she said, walking over to the crockpot.

"It's okay," Nicole said, putting Rashaad's plate down in front of him. He leaned over and kissed her in appreciation. Nicole blushed as Deniece cleared her throat.

"So the rumor is true?" she asked. Nicole playfully rolled her eyes.

"Baby, this is Sylar's aunt, Deniece. This is my man, Rashaad."

"Nice to meet you, man Rashaad," she teased. He chuckled but Nicole found nothing funny. Her and Deniece were not friendly like that.

"You need anything else?" Nicole asked. She heard Rashaad laugh under his throat before picking his fork up. Deniece shook her head before walking out the kitchen. "Ouch!"

Rashaad rubbed the spot on her butt that he'd just smacked. "You ain't have to do all that."

"I didn't do anything!" she said, shifting on her feet. He hugged her to his side while still eating with the other hand. "She needs to mind the business that pays her."

"So do you."

Nicole huffed before stepping away from his embrace. "I'm going to find my baby."

She could hear him chuckling as she walked out of the room. Her eyes roamed the room until they landed on her baby girl. She was terrorizing Pierre while Sage sat and laughed.

"You beating up your Uncle P, sugar baby?" Nicole asked, coming over and tickling her. She loved that Pierre took his uncle duties seriously, even though he was technically a second cousin.

"She's the cutest," Sage said.

"You ready for one?"

"Can we get married first?" Pierre cut in. Nicole playfully rolled her eyes.

"I wasn't talking to you."

"I kind of am though," Sage said, biting her lip as Pierre looked at her in shock. "What? It's Sylar's fault! She shouldn't be this cute!"

"On that note," Nicole said, taking Sylar from Pierre. "Gotta blast."

She heard them laugh as she settled Sylar on her hip and bounced her a little. She gripped her finger and swayed while making up a song. Sylar giggled.

"Aren't y'all cute."

Nicole sighed but kept her eyes and smile trained on her baby girl. "Hey ma."

Simone stood a little taller than her only daughter with half of her weight. She was always slim and reminded Nicole of it as much as she could. Her hair was black and in a low cut and Nicole tried to think of the last time she'd seen her with short hair...or seen her at all for that matter.

"Give me my grandbaby," Simone said, snatching Sylar out of her arm. Nicole frowned as Sylar fussed a little. Simone blew a raspberry on her and she giggled, wiggling around in her arms. Nicole's nerves relaxed a little but she still watched her.

"When did you get here?"

"Who is that man in the kitchen?" Simone ignored the question. "You need to be trying to get back with her father."

"We are both in relationships," Nicole said. "And even if we weren't...we were never together."

"Um," Simone said. "I thought I taught you better than that."

"Did you really?" Nicole asked, her patience wearing out. On cue, Marie walked over and playfully elbowed her sister.

"About time you got here. Waiting on you to sing happy birthday."

"Let me get her smash cake," Nicole said, quickly walking away. When she walked back into the kitchen, Rashaad was throwing his plate away. She tried to fix her face before he saw her, but it was too late.

"What's wrong, mama?" he asked, meeting her in front of the cake.

"Come on so you can meet my mom," she mumbled. Rashaad looked over her face before he nodded. "And I'm sorry in advance."

"What?" he asked.

"Ma," Nicole said, walking back into the living room. "This is Rashaad."

"She's getting fussy," Simone ignored her. "Come on and light these candles."

Rashaad frowned but quickly recovered before anyone else but Nicole could see. She took a deep breath and tried to hand the small cake to Julian, who walked over after Simone's announcement.

"No, she wants her daddy," Simone said, swiveling to give Julian access to take Sylar. Nicole gave a frustrated laugh before she turned to the decorated high chair. Raina came over to help her.

"Auntie is funny," she mumbled.

"Funny like a broken toe," Nicole replied. Raina laughed before she moved to let Julian put Sylar in the chair.

"What do we even say when we sing?" Pierre joked.

"Happy half birthday!" Nicole sang. Everyone chuckled before they actually started singing. Nicole winked at Rashaad who was recording. When Sylar realized everyone was looking at her, her bottom lip poked out and she reached for Nicole. "It's okay, sugar baby," she leaned down, letting Sylar touch her face. Once they finished singing she tried to stick her hand in the cake but Sylar quickly moved it away.

"She doesn't know what this is," Julian said, swiping at the icing. "Her momma won't let her have anything sweet," he teased.

"You agreed!" Nicole said, pouting. Julian smirked before holding his finger out for Sylar.

"I know, I'm just messing with you Nic," he said. "Try it baby girl."

Sylar stuck her neck out a little so her mouth was closer to his finger. Nicole watched as she licked it a little and then frowned. Julian tried it again and Sylar violently shook her head.

"Just take her picture then," Nicole said, sad for some reason. Rashaad chuckled in her ear before wrapping one arm around her waist to move his phone in front of her to get better pictures.

"You should be glad she doesn't want it," he whispered in her ear.

"Don't push my baby face in that cake!" Nicole said, seeing Simone step over to Sylar. She frowned but stepped back.

"What's your momma's deal?" Rashaad asked. Nicole shook her head.

"Long story."

The rest of the party went off without any more issues, but the fact that Simone was all of the sudden "team Harris" made Nicole's blood boil. She knew not to bring it up because her mother would make a big deal of it. So she let it go, hoping it wouldn't be brought up again.

chapter fourteen

"You look nice, when did you get your hair done?"

Nicole frowned, wondering where that came from. "A few days ago," she said, holding her hands out for Sylar.

Julian smiled and Nicole blinked, wondering why he was stalling. He'd called her several times while she was on the way so she figured he had something to do. "When you first loc'ed your hair I wasn't sure how it would go, but they fit you."

He had been extra nice to her since Sylar's half birthday party a couple of weeks ago. Nicole didn't forget that his woman wasn't there and she knew it was time to address it.

Nicole looked around Julian's place and sucked her teeth. "Where's Tessica?"

He frowned, rocking a sleeping Sylar in his arms. "Where did that come from?"

"I'd like to have a conversation with her soon," Nicole said. "If she's going to be around I think that's fair."

"That's not necessary," Julian responded. Nicole raised her eyebrow.

"Why wasn't she at the party? Did you tell her I didn't want her there or something? And why were you rude to Rashaad?"

"I was rude?" he asked. Nicole rolled her eyes before reaching for her baby. "Okay wait. Tessica and I broke up."

Nicole didn't respond but she was sure at that moment she really didn't care. She'd only asked because she saw no reason for him to be rude to Rashaad if he was also in a relationship. Actually, he had no reason to be rude since he hadn't wanted her in the first place.

"So you were rude to my man for what?"

"You could have warned me about him."

Nicole laughed hard, stepping back to put space between them so she wouldn't wake up Sylar with her loud outburst.

"I don't owe you anything, Julian."

"We broke up because she wasn't ready to be a step mother," he said, hurt filling his voice.

"Oh, you didn't fit into her box of perfect images huh?" Nicole said, tapping her index finger along her chin. "That sounds familiar."

Julian looked defeated and Nicole felt vindicated. He had ultimately taken back a woman who really wasn't for him to begin with. She felt almost an ounce of empathy for him but what he said next erased it all.

"I know I went about it wrong earlier in your pregnancy, but I really think we should give being a family a try. You're a great mother, Nicole. And..."

"I gotta go," she said, finally snatching Sylar from his hands. She cradled her against her chest to keep her from waking up before high tailing it out of Julian's front door.

Nicole felt a headache coming on as she drove away from Julian's place. She was meeting up with Raina at her aunt's house and she couldn't wait to tell them this tea. Julian had his damn nerve to think Nicole would go for that. It was bad enough the first time he tried his shotgun wedding attempt. Tessica would always come first to him and Nicole would never put herself in a position to be left for her again.

Sylar had woken up by the time she pulled in front of Marie's house. She was cranky and hungry but Marie took her as soon as they got in the house.

"Make her bottle," Marie said, bouncing her in her arms. "Why is your face red?"

"Y'all won't believe this," Nicole said, walking into the kitchen behind them. "Pour me a glass of that," she said, seeing Raina with a glass of wine.

"Oh Lord," she said, getting up to grab a glass. "What did Julian do now?"

Nicole sighed as she pulled the formula and cereal out of the diaper bag. "So I found out why the girlfriend wasn't at the party."

"Oh, I was waiting for this," Marie said. "Did he tell her not to come?"

"He probably didn't even tell her about the party."

"The girlfriend doesn't want to play step momma and left him… again!" Nicole said, shaking the bottle.

Raina laughed hard causing Sylar to look over at her. "You joking?"

"No," Nicole said. "And now he is trying to pull that family card again."

"He's a joke," Raina said. Marie just shook her head. Nicole noticed she was quiet and frowned.

"You think I should?"

"I didn't say that," she said.

"But what do you think?"

Nicole turned the hot water on the faucet and held the bottle under it.

"Momma," Raina said.

"I just think it's something to think about…for Sylar's sake."

"He takes care of her just fine without me allowing him to settle for me."

"She benefits more with a two-parent household."

"Wow," Raina said.

"I'm not saying you have to love him…"

Nicole's eyes widened before handing her the bottle. "All I went through to get out of this space that he mentally put me in and you'd want me to go back for the sake of my daughter…who is being cared for regardless. I can't believe you'd suggest that."

"Do you like how you grew up?" Marie asked, looking between her niece and daughter.

"That's not the same," Nicole said. "Our dads weren't around."

"…You're right," Marie said.

"And I have a man!" Nicole said, as if suddenly remembering another good point. "And I have no intentions on coming up off him."

"Oop!" Raina said, holding her glass out to toast her. Her and Nicole both giggled.

"So let me ask you this then," Marie said. "Why you so worked up about it?"

Nicole slumped in her seat before taking a sip of her wine. Why had Julian's admission worked her up so much? Was she not over him like she thought she was? Was she tripping by not considering his offer?

It was true that she never wanted a broken home. Watching everyone in her family go through that was hard for her. While most of them seemed to sweep it under the rug, Nicole always yearned for her traditional family. She wanted her first child to be her husband's first child. However, in the last few months, Nicole realized that would never be her reality. She wasn't sad about it anymore. It's just what it was.

She spent a little more time with her family before Sylar began to get fussy. Realizing it was close to her bedtime, Nicole said goodnight to her aunt and cousin and headed home. On the way, she got a call from Rashaad.

"I feel like I haven't heard from my woman all day," he teased. Nicole bit her lip as she slowly blinked.

"I'm sorry. I got caught up with my aunt and Rai."

"You okay?" he asked. "You sound different."

"Different how?" she asked, trying to change the octave in her voice.

"What's wrong?" he pressed.

"Nothing, I'm just tired," she halfway lied.

"You just left your aunt's?" he asked. Nicole told him that she had. "Come here. It's closer."

She sighed. "I have Sylar."

"You trust me?"

Nicole frowned but immediately answered. "Yes."

"Well, come on."

About ten minutes later, Nicole smiled as Rashaad walked down the short path of his house when she parked in his driveway. He opened her door as she turned the engine off, leaning over to kiss her before leaving her there and going around to the back door.

Nicole giggled. "Well, excuse me."

Rashaad smirked. "Get in the house."

Nicole raised her eyebrow, wondering why she liked his demanding side so much. She grabbed her purse and did as her man said, walking into the living room and waiting for him to bring Sylar in. After he closed the door and put the carseat down, Nicole went to lay Sylar's blanket on the couch but Rashaad stopped her.

"I finally cleaned the guest room out," he said. Nicole smiled.

"Oh, let me see," she said, bending down to pull Sylar from her carseat. Nicole thanked God she was still asleep. Walking down the hallway, she stepped aside while cuddling Sylar, waiting for Rashaad to open the guest room door. She eyed him when he looked back at her.

"What are you up to?" she asked. Nicole couldn't help but smile from his expression, but her smile dropped when he opened the door.

Instead of the bed that had been cluttered when she first saw his guest room, there was a smaller daybed with railing around it, a small dresser and a tv mounted on the wall. There was also a loveseat, a small bookshelf and nightstand in the corner. He'd put a few stuffed animals and what looked like a plug and play toy similar to the one Sylar had for tummy time.

Nicole couldn't form words.

"Your place is cool baby but I know that one bedroom is starting to stress you out," he teased. "Not saying you moving in or nothing, but I want both of yall to be comfortable here."

Nicole swallowed the lump in her throat and nodded, slowly walking over and placing Sylar in the middle of the bed, moving the pillows around her to give her space. She took a deep breath to calm her nerves as she waited a moment to make sure her baby stayed asleep. Walking past Rashaad, she grabbed his hand and pulled him out of the room. He said her name softly, but she ignored him, pulling him into his bedroom and shutting the door.

Nicole turned and grabbed his other hand, guiding him to sit on the edge of his bed before she backed up, kicking her shoes off.

"What are you doing?" he asked, watching her every move.

"Showing you how comfortable I am here," Nicole said as she pulled her shirt over her head.

chapter fifteen

Nicole looked devastated as Sylar tried to stand up on her own. Rashaad looked at her face and laughed.

"Mama."

"Leave me alone," she pouted. "She's walking already. It's too early."

"She's not walking," he said. "She's holding on to the couch. And she's ten months. I know babies who walked by then."

That made Nicole pout harder. Rashaad shook his head at her before holding his hand out behind Sylar's back just in case she fell. He was sitting on the floor with his back against the couch while Nicole laid across the couch, watching Sylar grip the edge of it and scoot between them. It was a Friday night and the couple was trying to decide if they wanted to go out or stay in once Julian came to pick Sylar up.

Nicole had to admit she was a little nervous for them to be in each other's space. It seemed as if ever since Julian told her about him and Tessica breaking up, his advances were more consistent. It had been over six months since she and Rashaad became official and things were going well. She didn't need any issues between them but she also didn't want to jeopardize Sylar's relationship with her dad. She hoped Julian would be respectful around Rashaad, but he was an asshole most days. With him, she could never be sure.

Sylar's hand landing on her mouth bought Nicole out of her thoughts. She puckered her lips and kissed the palm of her hand.

"You want to just stay in? I can cook and then we can do brunch tomorrow?" Nicole asked, idly trying to remember when the last time she went to brunch with Raina was.

"That's fine with me, mama."

Nicole smirked down at him, looking at his jaw slightly flex as he began to flip through channels. Her man was so fine to her. She caught herself watching him often when he wasn't paying attention. He'd always been handsome, but the care he put into their relationship made her feel obsessed at times. He was so considerate, but he stood his ground. He respected her boundaries with Sylar but made an effort to spend time with both of them and not just Nicole. She was really in love but not sure how to tell him that.

"Everything I say is fine with you," she teased. He slowly smirked before turning to look up at her.

"Don't make me sound like a simp," he said, leaning over. Nicole met him halfway for the kiss. A knock on the door caused him to sit up straight and Nicole to fall back on the couch. Rashaad made a move to stand up so Nicole hopped up, too.

"I got it," she said, standing on her toes to kiss his cheek. She grabbed Sylar in her arms, hoping since her things were at the door she could intercept Julian from saying anything crazy.

"There's my favorite girl," he said as Nicole opened the door. Sylar immediately let go of Nicole's shirt and reached for him. She leaned so far forward that Nicole had to step closer to Julian to keep her from falling before he grabbed her.

"Dang girl, your daddy ain't leaving you," she said, playfully tapping Sylar's shoulder before tickling her.

"Say, don't be a hater all your life, momma."

Nicole rolled her eyes before reaching for the bag. "We had to switch her formula so I got two cans for you to start."

He frowned. "What happened? That's what the doctor said yesterday?" he asked.

Nicole nodded. "They said it wasn't major but her spitting up could be an allergy so she said switch to the soy kind to see if it helps."

He nodded before taking the bag. "Where's that damn cow at?"

Nicole frowned, not seeing the small stuffed cow attached to her binkie string on her outfit. "Must be in the living room. I'll be right back."

Julian followed Nicole into the living room and she silently cursed.

"What's up, man?" Julian said, slightly chuckling. Rashaad was on the couch by now, watching television so he didn't take notice of Julian's tone.

"What's up?"

Nicole searched the couch before finding the pacifier. "Here it is. Goodbye."

"Dang," Julian said, laughing. Nicole rolled her eyes before leaning over to kiss Sylar all over her face. "Think about what I said," Julian said, stepping closer to Nicole to try and whisper. Nicole ignored it, hoping Rashaad hadn't heard it and Julian would let it go.

"See you Monday, sugar baby," Nicole said as she continued to kiss Sylar's face. She giggled before attaching herself to her dad's arm. Neither of them noticed that Rashaad was definitely tuned into the interaction and heard everything. He pushed his back into the couch, trying to calm his nerves. He knew that Julian had been taking shots at him from day one, not respecting his position in Nicole's life at all. He thought she was way too nice. Julian didn't have boundaries when it came to how he moved and that bothered Rashaad. He had no intentions of trying to take his place as Sylar's dad, but Julian had to know that Rashaad had weight, too.

"He's acting bipolar," she mumbled, walking back in after seeing them out. Rashaad hadn't moved from his seat on the couch. "Did you decide what you wanted to eat?"

"What is he talking about, Nicole?"

"Hum? I didn't hear anything."

He huffed while looking up at the ceiling. "I know you not about to try and lie to me. What do you need to think about?"

"Nothing," she said, quickly. "Absolutely nothing we need to care about."

He frowned. "It's something. You're lying."

"It's not that big of a deal," she said, trying to place her hands on his chest. He stepped back and her heart dropped.

"It went from nothing to not that big of a deal real quick," he said, shaking his head.

"Promise you won't get mad?"

"I won't get mad at you if you didn't do anything to jeopardize what we got going on."

Nicole's shoulder slumped as he realized that accusation hurt her feelings. He wanted to comfort her but needed his question answered first. Clearing up any confusion was the priority.

"He's single and basically attempted to be family again."

"What you mean again? Y'all were never together right? Ain't that what you told me?"

Nicole slowly nodded. "When he found out I was pregnant he tried to be on some shotgun wedding stuff."

"And now what? You're down with that?"

Nicole frowned but kept her tone soft. "Baby, you know that's not what I want."

"Do I?" he asked, attempting to get up. Nicole shook her head before grabbing his arm.

"Don't do that," she said, trying to remain calm. She could tell his emotion was misplaced and that kept her calm. Nicole had never been so in tune with someone as she was with Rashaad. It scared her at first, but now she realized how much of a gift it was. In any other situation, she would have been upset and ready to argue, but she could tell he was afraid. Even if that fear had no legs to stand on, Nicole wouldn't invalidate that feeling.

"Don't have me out here looking stupid," he said, moving her hand but not getting up from the couch. "If you want this nigga just say that." She felt her skin getting hot as he continued to go off. "I told you I wasn't playing this game with you. Didn't I?"

Realizing he wanted an answer, she nodded. "I'm not playing with you. I love you."

"Nicole," he said in a warning tone. She tried to contain her smile before she straddled his lap. Rashaad dropped his hands to his sides, but she picked them up and wrapped them around her body before wrapping hers around his neck. She kissed along his jaw, chin and neck until she felt his body relax.

"I love you," she repeated in between kisses. "You're my man right?" He nodded. "You take real good care of my heart?" He nodded. "You take damn good care of my body?" He nodded, pressing his fingers into her back. "Do you leave any room for another man in my mind?"

Rashaad looked down at her and bit his lip. "I do all that?" he teased, pressing his lips to hers but not kissing her. Nicole nodded before sticking her tongue in his mouth. He let her control the kiss for a little while before lifting his right hand to her neck. Nicole gasped as she felt her air flow construct just enough to heighten the rest of her senses. "I'm tripping?"

"Just a little," she said, smirking as he finally smiled. "But it just lets me know that you value what you have."

"Um," he said, biting her bottom lip. "Let me show you how much."

Nicole squealed as he suddenly got up, securing her in his arms, and walked back towards her bedroom. She clasped her hands behind his neck and smiled, giddily. He chuckled at her energy.

"You know I love you, too. Right?" He asked, licking his lips. Nicole nodded without hesitation, pecking his lips over and over until he finally got to the bedroom. "You make sure he keeps being somebody I ain't gotta worry about."

"You ain't gotta worry about nobody," she replied quickly. She kissed his chin, making sure to look into his eyes as she repeated herself. If it was one thing she never wanted him to question, it was her devotion to him. She didn't want to get too emotional at that moment, but he had been everything she ever prayed for. Although she could be love struck at times, Nicole was not a dummy. She knew she had a good man and she was determined not to let anything she did jeopardize that.

Her back hitting her bed brought her back to the moment.

"You're beautiful, baby," he said, untwisting the tie of her fluffy robe. Nicole smirked up at him as she pulled on the end of his shirt.

"Yeah?" she whispered. Rashaad looked down at her and licked his lips. "Enough to kiss my feet?" The frown on his face caused her to laugh.

"Why are you so goofy?" he asked, wrapping his hand around her left ankle.

"I was just playing," she said, moving her foot to spread her legs. He shook his head before he finished removing her robe and his clothes.

Not feeling like foreplay at that moment, Rashaad stuck his thumb in Nicole's mouth. She licked around it for a second before he removed it and rubbed between her thighs. She pulled his locs down so she could kiss him and within seconds he was inside of her.

"Slow down," she whined. Rashaad shook his head before leaning back enough to pull her left ankle in front of his face. Nicole whined at the bend in her knee but instantly moaned as he stuck her toes in his mouth. "Rashaad!"

"Um?" he groaned, kissing her big toe before sticking it back in his mouth, not changing up his rhythm even a little bit. Nicole's eyes shut as she tried to control her breathing.

"I can't stand you," she groaned. He kissed her ankle before letting it go.

"You'll be alright," he chuckled, pushing harder and faster while kissing her neck. Nicole was sure that was worse than her foot being in his mouth.

chapter sixteen

Realizing that Rashaad was still a little insecure in their relationship made Nicole want to prove her loyalty. Since his birthday was coming up, she decided she would throw him a surprise party. Gathering all of his close friends and family in one place to show him love. He deserved it for all the things he did for everyone else. Well, Nicole couldn't speak for anyone else... but he did a lot of her.

It was almost like she didn't have to ask for anything. If her man thought she needed something, he took care of it. He might as well have been her landlord with all of the things he'd fixed in her apartment. He never came over empty handed, even when Nicole begged him to. He'd still show up with a bottle of wine or something for Sylar. She thought a birthday party would be a perfect way to show him how much she cared. Her only problem was figuring out who to invite.

After confirming that he didn't have any plans the weekend before his birthday, Nicole took a risk and reached out to his mother. Although she thought it was a good idea and promised not to tell, she wasn't much help when it came to who to invite. Rashaad had introduced Nicole to only a few of his friends, who he claimed were the only important ones. She didn't have any of their numbers, so she went through her man's friends list on social media.

Nicole jumped when her phone rang while she was sending one of them a message.

"Hey baby," she said, answering but going back to her app.

"What you doing, mama?"

"Waiting for Sylar to wake up," she halfway lied. "How's work?"
"Almost done with this site," he said. Nicole frowned, hoping she'd have more time. "What's for dinner?"
"Can we go out?" she asked. "I want seafood."
"Sounds like the move," he said. Nicole finished sending the message before a slow smile spread across her face.
"You so good to me, baby."
He chuckled. "You being extra over some food, Nic. You eat today?"
"No...but that's not the point." They both laughed. "I just like how you care for me."
"...Stop talking sweet before I leave work early."
She giggled. "You are always trying to leave work early. Don't put that on me."
"I'm always trying to get to you, mama," he said as his background got louder. "Let me finish this. I'll let you know when I'm on my way to get y'all."
"Love you," Nicole sang. She waited until he responded before disconnecting the call. She smiled to see his friend, Ayden, had responded to her message. He said he'd handle the guest list on that end if she just sent him details.
About an hour before Rashaad got off work, Nicole got her and Sylar cleaned and dressed for their little date night. She still hadn't introduced many different foods, but Sylar loved french fries so she knew she'd be happy when they got to the restaurant. Since she hadn't spent much time with her man that week, Nicole packed their overnight bag and put it next to Sylar's diaper bag by the door. Rashaad chuckled when he came in and saw it.
"I take it y'all staying with me tonight?" he asked. Nicole nodded before following him outside to his truck. "You probably got enough stuff over there."
"I always end up leaving something I need, too," she pouted after they got settled in the car.
"When is your lease up?" he asked. Nicole felt her heart jump.
"A few months," she said, frowning. "Why?"
"I know you want something bigger. You thought about moving in with me?"
Nicole blinked as Rashaad kept his eyes on the road. She swallowed the lump in her throat before clearing it. "I mean..not really."
"Damn."

"I didn't mean it like that," she said. "I just...I don't know."

She could tell by the tension in his jaw that he didn't like her response, but she kept quiet because she wasn't sure what to say. In fact, she didn't say anything for a while. When they got to the restaurant, Sylar was asleep. Rashaad held her until she woke up, putting her in a high chair once her fries came.

"Are you mad?" she whispered. Rashaad shook his head. "So why aren't you talking?"

"You aren't talking either."

"I don't want you to be mad."

"So explain to me what we're doing."

Nicole took a deep breath before she nodded. "I love you."

He relaxed a little. "I know that."

"I don't want to be a live-in girlfriend." Rashaad just looked at her. "I am completely in love with you, but I've seen how this works. I want to be married. I want to live with my husband. I don't want to look up 10 years from now and be in a common law marriage, baby. That's not what I see for us."

Nicole bit her lip and watched him process what she'd just said. She took a deep breath before asking what was really on her mind. "Do you...do you want to be married...to me. Like not today but in the future...not like too far though."

"Mama," he said, cutting her off. "Let me answer."

Nicole blushed in embarrassment. "Sorry."

"I do want to marry you," he said. Nicole wanted to melt. "We ain't had that conversation so that's my bad. I don't want you to feel pressed. I just knew you weren't comfortable in that apartment. I got space. I'm programmed to fix shit for you. That's just how twisted you got my heart, mama. I still want you with me, but if you want to wait then we'll wait. I told you I'm not going nowhere."

Nicole slouched in her seat, leaning forward to hold herself up with the edge of the table. "How did I get so lucky?"

"You blessed, baby," he said, licking his lips as a fire lit in his eyes. "I'm proud of you for communicating the way you did. That's grown woman shit."

"You make it easy," she said, biting her lip.

"Um... Come here."

Nicole giggled. "No."

"You better lean over this table and kiss me."

"You don't know how to act in public," she said.

"Your fault."

Nicole gasped as he reached over and grabbed her shirt, balling it up in his fist as he made her meet him halfway over the table for a kiss.

"You're so embarrassing!" she teased, sitting back and helping Sylar reach more of her fries. "I love it."

Rashaad laughed wholeheartedly before he continued his meal.

A few days later found Nicole almost regretting her decision not to move in with her man. She sighed as Sylar finally went down for her nap, but the headache pounding on the side of her face kept her from relaxing. All she wanted to do was sleep as well but she had work to do. Although most of the planning for Rashaad's party was done, she wanted to go over the details before he got to her place that night. She also had other work to do. She'd been fed up with her work position and wanted to finally get into HR. Her current job had no openings, so she began looking elsewhere.

It was frustrating because she'd done all the work in school and couldn't break 40k a year. How was that fair? She'd done what she was supposed to do by getting an education. Finding a job in her field shouldn't have been this hard. Wanting to give up and just work her job had been on her mind, but the little girl curled up in her bed made her think otherwise. So, instead of taking a nap, she went into the living room and pulled her laptop open.

While she was searching, Rashaad came in from work, finally using the key she'd given him weeks ago. She made sure all her internet tabs were closed that had anything to do with the party before watching him walk in from the foyer. He was a little dirty from whatever job site he was on, so he only leaned over to kiss Nicole's forehead.

"What's up, mama? No food today?" he asked.

"Didn't feel like cooking," she groaned.

"You should have told me to pick something up," he said while walking towards her bedroom.

"It slipped my mind. Don't wake her up please."

Rashaad nodded before changing directions to go to the bathroom. Nicole smirked but kept working. After a while, all the jobs she saved started to look the same. It was discouraging filling out so many. She heard a door close just as some music started playing. Nicole looked up to see Rashaad, now clean and shirtless, walking towards her with his phone in hand. She tried to hold her smile in as she recognized the melody.

"Don't you start," she said. Rashaad ignored her and put his phone down on the table before sliding the laptop off her lap and making her stand up.

Rashaad sang along with D'Angelo as he pulled Nicole's arms around his neck before immediately rubbing her butt.

She giggled. "You can't sing, love."

"So what?" he said before he continued. Nicole relaxed in his arms as he swayed them side to side. Taking a deep breath, she rubbed his neck with her thumbs as she lay her head on his shoulder. His scent was like eucalyptus to her. He didn't smell like it, but it calmed her just the same.

Rashaad's fingertips gripped the flesh on her hips as he sighed into her neck. "Stop stressing, mama," he assured her. "The right one will come."

Nicole started to whine. "I'm tired of waiting." She swallowed a moan when he smacked her behind.

"You know we don't do all that whining," he said, leaning back to look in her eyes. "You trust me?"

Nicole gave him a breathless yes as his hand traveled up and around her neck. "I do."

Rashaad looked into her eyes for a moment before he smiled, licking his lips in satisfaction that her answer was the truth. "You want to quit until you find what you want? I can cover your bills. Or you want to thug it out?"

Nicole felt her knees get weak. Even after she rejected his proposal to move in, her man was still trying to fix her problems. "I can thug it out, baby."

"You what?" he asked, smirking as his grip tightened a little. This time she couldn't stop the moan from pushing past her lips. "Focus, mama."

"How sway?" she yelled. Rashaad laughed before releasing her neck and wrapping her up in his arms. "Um," she hummed. "It's so safe here."

"You better damn know it," he said. Nicole smiled before she kissed him. "You gonna tell me what you got planned for next weekend?" Nicole kept smiling as she kissed him again. Once she was satisfied she shook her head. Rashaad playfully pushed her away from him and she laughed, trying to get back into his arms. "Nope. You don't love me for real."

Nicole pouted, holding her arms out. "I promise I do," she said, looking up at him with doe eyes. Rashaad bit his lip before reaching for her hand. Nicole smiled at how quickly he folded. She couldn't gloat because she wanted to live in his skin at this point. "And I promise the surprise will be worth it."

"I don't doubt that," he said, eyeing her up and down. Faint cries could be heard as their little bubble was sweetly invaded. "I'll get baby girl. Order us some food."

"I'ma marry him," Nicole thought as she sat back on the couch and pulled up Door Dash on her phone. *"And give him a lot of babies."*

chapter seventeen

"I can't believe you're throwing this man a party," Raina said, straightening out a rounded tablecloth. "This is your problem now."

Nicole gasped before looking over at her cousin. She was a few tables away fixing a centerpiece. "What's my problem? I thought you liked him?"

"I do, but this is a bit much," Raina complained. Nicole bit her lip as she twisted the 8 ball centerpiece. She themed it around billiards and pool since that was one of Rashaad's hobbies. She tried to go simple with the decorations but didn't want it to look cheap. Nicole stepped back to look around at the small venue she rented out and sighed. She initially planned a small get together with his family, but there were now 50 people on the list so she had to accommodate that.

"Ugh, forget I said anything," Raina said. "It looks nice." Nicole rolled her eyes before throwing a pen at her. Raina dodged it before looking at her watch. "What time do you need to get the cake?"

"Now, let's go."

Nicole told the owner of the venue she'd be back when it was time for the DJ to set up. Rashaad was Facetiming her before she could leave.

"Hi lover," she smiled into the camera, almost laughing at the frown on his face.

"Why did I wake up alone?" he asked. Nicole bit her lip.

"I had to pick up something," she said. "I'll be back in a minute." Rashaad got quiet. "You need anything?" He didn't respond. Nicole laughed. "Really baby? I want to say it in person."

"You can only say it once?" he asked. Nicole grinned.

"Happy birthday, my love! You want me to sing?" She cleared her throat.

"Nah," he said, quickly. "But come back so I can make you sing."

"Oh, you just hating," she said, trying to ignore the rest of his statement. "I'll be there soon." She looked up to see Raina mouthing for her to get off the phone so they could finish. "Love you."

"Love you, more."

Nicole made sure the phone call was disconnected before sliding it into her purse. "Can you go get the cake?"

"No! How are you going to put me to work so you can go be nasty?"

"Please, Rai? I owe you! It's just down the street," Nicole begged. "I'll pay for your next nail appointment."

Raina frowned. "Fine. I want that in writing," she said, pointing at Nicole. "Text her and tell her I'm coming."

Nicole kissed Raina's cheek before she picked up her purse and headed out the building. She sent a text to the baker that Raina was picking the cake up. She was the same one who made Sylar's half birthday cake so she was familiar with them. She pulled up to her man's place about twenty minutes later. Nicole giggled when he met her at the door.

"Happy birthday," she sang as he wrapped one arm around her waist, closing and locking the door before pulling her back to his bedroom. His skin was slick and he only had sweats on so Nicole figured he'd just taken a shower. She pressed her lips into his chest before biting it.

"I didn't like waking up by myself on my birthday," he said, pulling at her leggings. Nicole's stomach flipped as she helped him get her clothes off. She turned towards the bed and sat down, Rashaad standing up in front of her as she pulled his sweats down.

"I'm sorry," she whispered. She swallowed the saliva in her mouth as she looked up at him. His locs were hanging freely around his chest and shoulders as he looked down at her with a heat that she felt deep in her core. He bit his lip as he ran his thumb over her bottom lip, moving his locs out of the way with his other hand. Nicole giggled as they fell right back in his face. She looked over his face and sighed, gripping his side to move him closer.

"I got you something," he said. She blinked a few times before looking in his eyes.

"What? It's your birthday, baby."

"I know that," he said. "I can do what I want on my birthday." She smiled. "Yes, you can. Give it to me then."

"Give you what?" he said, his voice lower as he finally moved to lay on top of her.

"You play too much," she said, wrapping her legs around him.

"I did get you something else," he said. "Just not sure which one I want to give you first."

"Can I pick?" she said, biting at his chin before kissing him. He shook his head. "Which one will I like more?" The look on his face made her laugh.

"The other one," he mumbled against her neck.

"Which one will you like more?" she said, closing her eyes.

"Probably the other one, too."

"...Well, save the best for last."

"Bet," he said, quickly. He pushed his knee between her thighs to spread her legs. Nicole's laughs soon turned into moans.

An hour later, the couple had taken a shower and were quickly getting dressed. Nicole still had some things to set up and luckily Rashaad had a hair appointment that would allow her time.

"What are you about to do?" he asked, hugging her to his chest. He had been overly affectionate the last few days, but Nicole wasn't complaining.

"Raina's going to style my hair for me for dinner," she said. He nodded while looking over her features. "Baby, what's up? Can I get my gift now? I want later to be all about you."

He smiled. "You sure?"

"Yes," she said, pouting. Rashaad kissed her forehead before moving over to open the top drawer of his dresser. Nicole smiled, thinking it was jewelry, but her smile dropped when she saw how small the box was.

Rashaad cleared his throat as he turned to her. "I thought about a hundred different ways to do this. I had settled on doing it as soon as we woke up, but you were gone." Nicole tried to remember to breathe as he walked closer to her. "I thought about doing something big with all your family, but I know you don't like to ugly cry in front of people...and I didn't want you to feel pressured to say yes." Nicole frowned from that last comment. "You asked me the other day what I really wanted for my birthday and I really want you to be my wife," he said as he opened the box. "Marry me?"

He was in front of her now, their foreheads touching. Nicole watched the rapid rise and fall of his chest, the only indication that he was nervous. Her ears began to ring as he lifted his hand to her cheek, raising her head so that he could look into her eyes. He kissed her, soft and short, before repeating his question. Nicole closed her eyes and nodded.

"That's not going to work, mama," he whispered against her lips, kissing her again.

"Yes," she said, putting her hand on top of his.

"Yeah?"

"Yes, baby," she said, opening her eyes again. His smile made her feel like she was floating. He kissed her again before putting the ring on her finger.

"You don't think it's too soon?" she asked, looking at the ring.

"You just said yes," he said. Nicole giggled.

"You know what I mean," she said, wrapping her arms around his neck. Even though she was nervous, she smiled at his happiness.

"We don't have to get married tomorrow," he said, pushing his fingers into the back of her thighs. "I just wanted you to be my fiance on my birthday."

Nicole smiled harder. "This isn't fair. Now my gift won't seem as good."

He laughed before kissing her. "I already know you're throwing me a party."

Nicole gasped before she moved out of his arms and frowned. "Who told you? Ayden."

He grinned but didn't confirm. "I'll act surprised, mama," he said, trying to pull her back into his embrace. Nicole pouted and tried to swatch his hand away. He frowned before wrapping his hand around the back of her neck to keep her still. Nicole groaned as he kissed her hard.

"I'm sorry baby," she said, kissing him back. "I just wanted to do something nice for you."

Rashaad's smile was different this time. His eyes swept over her face before using his thumbs to caress her cheeks.

"You're nice for me."

Since the surprise was ruined, Nicole planned to go back to Rashaad's place after making sure everything was ready for the party. She called to check on Sylar, who was with her aunt, before heading out to meet Raina at the venue so they could make sure the food was set up properly. She couldn't wait to tell Raina about the proposal, but Nicole decided she wouldn't tell anyone else until after the party. She truly wanted tonight to be about her man.

Her man. Her fiancé. Nicole smiled at the thought of being able to say that. She had been on autopilot the last hour. She'd made sure to wear his favorite color but didn't do too much. She was putting the finishing touches on her makeup when he came back home. He didn't get his locs retwisted a lot because he liked them full, but he did get them done for his birthday. He had flat twists in the front and two strand twists in the back. Nicole loved when his locs hung freely, but this style framed his face well.

"I look good, baby?" he teased, kissing her forehead to knock her out of her thoughts. She blushed before pushing him away.

"Get in the shower please."

"Party don't start until I get there, mama," he said, eyeing her before moving towards the bathroom.

"The party started 20 minutes ago," she said. "Gotta make sure everyone is there before you."

"You know somebody's still going to miss the surprise," he said. They both laughed. "Iron my shirt for me?"

"Alright done," she said, pointing to the bed.

"Okay, she's on her wifely duties already."

Nicole playfully rolled her eyes before turning back to the mirror on his dresser. Ayden called while Rashaad was in the shower.

"I heard you spilled the beans," she said.

He laughed. "My fault, sis. It's packed in here though."

Nicole sighed. She was never a fan of her man's friends or family calling her sis. It always went sour once the relationship ended. She hated fake loyalty. "Good. I'll let you know when we're outside."

It was almost 8 when the couple pulled up. Nicole took a deep breath, not sure why she was even nervous now that the secret was out. She honestly just wanted everything to go right. This was also a chance for her to meet the rest of the people that were important in his life. She waited for him to turn the car off before pulling a blindfold out of her clutch. Rashaad frowned before he shook his head.

"We're not doing that," he said. Nicole pouted.

"You said you'd play along!"

"Put your hand over my eyes then," he said.

"You're taller than me."

"You got on heels."

Nicole pouted harder. He frowned while she held her ground. Rashaad sighed before running his hand down his face. Nicole smiled at her impending victory. Once they got out of the car, Nicole made her way behind him to put it on.

"You're so sweet and handsome," she said, moving the band under his locs so it would sit comfortably on his face. "You're so good to me." She yelped when he suddenly pulled her around to his front and kissed her hard while smacking her butt. Nicole moaned when one of his hands gripped her neck.

"Don't play with me out here."

Tightening her core to keep her from falling over, she grinned before opening her eyes to kiss him one more time.

"Come on, Mr. Baptiste."

Once they made their way into the building and down the hall, Nicole paused at the double doors before Ayden and Raina appeared. Once the doors opened, Rashaad went into action.

"Mama, you know I don't like surprises," he said, reaching around with the hand Nicole wasn't holding. "Where we at and why is it so quiet?"

Nicole giggled before she stepped around to grab the cake from Raina who already had the candles lit. Ayden stepped behind Rashaad and waited until Nicole nodded to pull the blindfold off.

"SURPRISE!"

Nicole held in her laugh as the DJ started playing the birthday song and Rashaad tried to act surprised. He smiled at her as everyone closed in and sang before he blew out the candles. He turned to wrap his arm around her waist and kiss her forehead as his mom walked over with a mic in her hand.

"Don't start all that," she teased! "Happy birthday to my favorite son! Can't believe I'm only 50 with a 40 year old."

"Ma," Rashaad said. "That makes you look bad."

"It makes me look young," she said, swatting his hand. "Anyway. Enjoy your night. We are all here to celebrate you and your life. I'm proud of the man you turned out to be. I love you!"

Everyone aww'd as the photographer Nicole hired took pictures of Rashaad kissing his mom's cheek and hugging her. Raina nudged her before taking the cake.

"How old is she for real? Because she could pass for 50," she whispered.

Nicole giggled. "He said she had him at 18."

"Okay, momma," Raina said. They both laughed before walking over towards the dessert table to put the cake in its place. "Everything came out nice. I been trying to figure out who this woman is though."

Nicole frowned. "What woman?"

Raina nodded her head in the direction of one of the round tables. Nicole's eyes followed the path until she landed on a woman and a teenager at a table with one of Rashaad's female cousins. She hadn't seen her before so she wasn't sure if she was a cousin or a family friend. The woman was slim from what Nicole could tell from her sitting down. She had smooth dark skin but a small patch under her eye was a little lighter than the rest of her face. Her lashes fluttered as she laughed at something and patted the girl's hair down.

"I don't know," Nicole finally said. "Ayden handled the list."

Raina rolled her eyes. "He's a hoe."

Nicole's eyes widened as she finally took her eyes off the mystery woman and looked at her cousin.

"You know him?"

"No, but he tried me right before his woman came in with his momma," Raina said, shaking her head. "I should tell."

"Don't start any drama at my man's party," Nicole said, swatting her arm. Raina caught her hand and Nicole immediately tried to pull away.

"Don't play with me," Raina said, smiling. "What is this? Nicole Ariana!"

"Don't do that," Nicole said, finally getting her hand back. "It just happened. I was going to tell you after the party."

"You tell me the moment something like this happens!" Raina said. Nicole laughed at her excitement. "I need a blunt. This is going to make me cry."

"Really? You seem to think I was doing too much for his party earlier," Nicole said, giving her cousin a side eye.

"Yeah, too much for your boyfriend. Not your fiance!"

Nicole laughed. "Well, hush. He wants to tell his mom first so keep your voice down."

Raina clamped her hand down on her mouth before dancing a little to whatever the DJ was playing. Nicole shook her head. The song switched and Raina pushed her back towards Rashaad.

"Your man wants you," she said. Nicole giggled before dancing back over to him.

"It looks good in here, mama," he said, wrapping her up in his arms. She exhaled while looking up at him, running her thumb over his bottom lip. "You gonna play me later?" he asked, referring to the pool table. "We can bet."

"That's not cute. You know I can't play," she pouted. He looked over her face before biting his lip.

"I'll make the bet good..."

Nicole bit her lip but before she could respond, Ayden came and broke them up.

"Stop cupcaking and come kick it with your people."

"Nigga..."

"No babe," Nicole said, smiling as she patted his chest. "He's right. I'm going to go chat with your mom for a while."

"See, she letting you off the leash."

Nicole rolled her eyes before walking off before she said something crazy to Ayden. She found Miss Diane.

"You did good," she said, patting the seat next to her. "He looks happy."

"Does he?" Nicole said, biting her lip. "Good."

"Girl hush, you know my son is in love," she said. "And I heard just how much. Congratulations."

Nicole blushed. "Thank you."

Diane turned to the person next to her. "This is my oldest cousin, Shyann."

"Rashaad calls you Aunt Shy Shy?" Nicole asked. She nodded.

"That's me. Nice to meet you. And why are we congratulating you?" she asked. Miss Diane held up Nicole's left hand. "Oop! Okay nephew!"

"I didn't think he would tell everyone so soon," Nicole said, feeling her face get hot. "I wanted tonight to be about him."

"He's probably telling because ..."

"Shut up, Shy," Miss Diane said, hitting her knee. "He told me as soon as he hit the door. He can't hold nothing from his momma."

Nicole frowned, wondering what that was about. "Well, if he's okay with telling people then it's all good."

"You want a big wedding?"

Nicole shrugged. "I'm with whatever he's with," she said, honestly. Both women raised an eyebrow before looking at each other.

"I see why he loves you," Shyann said. "He said you have a baby?"

Nicole nodded. "She'll be one soon. I'll probably cry."

"That's young. What does her daddy think about you and my nephew?"

"Damn, Shyann," Miss Diane said. Nicole was glad she said it. She wasn't even really his aunt to be asking all these questions.

"It's fine, Miss Diane," Nicole replied. "Her father is active but he knows his boundaries. We've been over since before she was born. My man doesn't do drama and neither do I."

"Oh, well...that's good to know."

Nicole looked around the room to see Ayden pulling Rashaad over to the table where the mystery woman and the teenager were. Rashaad looked a little apprehensive but smiled when the girl jumped up and ran over to hug him. Nicole slightly smiled at the interaction because of how happy the girl seemed. Nicole felt her heart drop and wondered where the anxiety came from as she watched on. The woman looked up at Rashaad and said something, but he ignored her and continued to interact with the girl, opening her gift and smiling down at her. He kissed her forehead before hugging her again. The woman said something else but he ignored her again before walking away.

"Miss Diane, do you know who that is?" Nicole blurted out, not being able to hold it in.

Miss Diane bit her lip. When Shyann saw that she wasn't answering, she took it upon herself to.

"That's Chanel. You never heard of her?"

Nicole frowned. "Why would I have?"

Before she could answer, the girl ran over and jumped into Diane's arms, rocking the table a little.

"Be careful, Imani," Miss Diane laughed. "I missed you, too."

"I missed you the most, Nana D!"

Nana D?

Nicole was fuming as she began to put two and two together. She swayed in her seat as she looked up and met the gaze of her fiance as he began walking over to the table. She had to remember to breathe as the girl kept talking.

"I didn't think Momma was going to let us come but I'm so glad I got to see you and give daddy a gift."

"Daddy?" Nicole yelled. Everyone in ear shot looked at her as Rashaad stopped in his tracks.

The girl nodded before looking up at Rashaad. "Daddy, is this her? She's pretty like you said. I'm Imani. Nice to meet you."

Nicole felt Miss Diane tap her side, knocking her out of her shocked state. "Ni..Nice to meet you, too, Imani. I um...I have to go check on something."

"Mama," Rashaad called after her as she quickly got up from the table. "Nicole, wait."

Rashaad rushed and stood in front of her just as she got to the double doors. She turned and frantically looked for Raina, who was already getting her purse and heading her way. She sighed before turning back to leave.

"Your best bet is to get out my way."

"Let me explain," he said, trying to grab her shoulders. "I didn't know they'd be here."

Nicole huffed. "I'm not doing this with you right now. Get out of my way."

"What's the rush?" she heard a voice from behind say. "We haven't met yet."

Nicole watched Rashaad's body tense up as he pulled her to him but looked over her. She had never seen that expression on his face but she really didn't want him touching her at the moment.

"Chanel, back up."

When she heard the name, Nicole spun around to face the woman. She held her hand up to stop Raina from moving closer. She hated that everyone was now watching them but this was Rashaad's fault for not letting her leave.

"What would we need to meet for?" Nicole asked. "I wasn't aware you existed."

"You know now though, right?" Chanel said, smirking. "Just in case you don't, I'm Chanel, Rashaad's wife."

If he hadn't been behind her, Nicole was sure she would have stumbled into the wall.

"Ex-wife," he said, quickly. "Don't pull that shit here. Why are you even here?"

Chanel frowned. "I'm here because our daughter wanted to celebrate your birthday. Since you've seemed to have forgotten about her. She never sees you now."

"Did you tell her why she doesn't see me? Or are you content with the lie you tell everybody else?"

Nicole roughly swatted his hand away from her waist before moving from between them.

"You two obviously have shit to discuss that does not concern me. Raina, let's go."

"Nicole," Rashaad tried to stop her again. She pushed him just as the tears finally broke.

"No!" she yelled. "I don't care what this is right now. The fact that I have to find out like this. Like you didn't have every opportunity to explain it to me makes me realize all the shit you said you were was a lie."

"Baby, don't do that," he pleaded.

She shook her head. "You don't get to talk to me right now! I wouldn't believe shit you said anyway." She looked him up and down and shook her head, wondering if anything he'd ever said to her was true. "Enjoy your party."

chapter eighteen

Two weeks. Nicole was back to counting time in weeks, but these were not as fun as before.

It had been two weeks since she found out about Chanel and Imani and she could honestly say she wished she never did. Although she was ignoring his calls, Rashaad left several voicemails explaining the situation, but it felt too late.

They were high school sweethearts who just grew apart but reconnected as adults. Chanel was in an abusive relationship but the guy went to jail when Imani was five. By the time Imani was nine, Rashaad and Chanel had fallen back in love and gotten married. Apparently, when Imani's dad got out of jail, Chanel cheated on Rashaad with him. He found out after a few months and filed for divorce. That was four years ago. He hadn't stopped taking care of Imani, but their relationship was strained. At first it was because her biological dad didn't want Imani around Rashaad. However, he ended up back in jail. Rashaad thought he'd be able to see Imani more, but now Chanel was upset because Rashaad wanted nothing to do with her.

This was all from his mouth. At this point he could say the sky was blue and Nicole wouldn't believe it.

"He could have told me he was married," she whispered, shaking her head as she looked down at the roses he'd sent. "How could he even think to propose to me without telling me that!" She heard Raina grunt and she rolled her eyes. "What?"

"So...I looked it up. Divorce is public record. It was finalized like four years ago. And did you ever ask him if he was married before?"

"And?" Nicole said, frowning. "She's still an ex...an ex-wife at that! Who knows what could happen. What if I go through with this and go all in with this man and she decides to come back huh? Where does that leave me then? It was too soon for this anyway."

Raina smirked. "Oh..that's what this is about."

Nicole pushed her back into the couch and groaned, her eyes on the ring she'd taken off and put on the coffee table. "How am I supposed to just trust that he's different?" More tears fell. "I want to...I just."

"Nicole," Raina said, sternly. "You aren't dumb. Look at the difference. Did Julian ever commit to you? Or even mention commitment?" Nicole shook her head. "Did he make you wait to get physical because he wanted to fully get to know you first?" She shook her head again. "Did he make it a priority to talk to you even when he was busy?"

"Okay, I get it."

"I don't think you do," Raina said, rocking Sylar in her arms. "This is all what you've told me that Rashaad has done yet you claim you don't know he's different. Nevermind the fact that you played him first and he still took it there with you. Nothing about how that man moves mimics your baby daddy. Just admit you're scared."

"I'm scared as hell!" Nicole said without hesitation. They both laughed.

"Real talk cousin," Raina said. "Which one you more scared of? This love being real or being alone and paranoid for the rest of your life? That man really being done with you?"

The air left Nicole's body as she thought about Rashaad really moving on. The thought of it alone hurt more than seeing Julian with Tessica.

"I don't want him to be done," she whispered. Raina smiled. "But I need him to prove it."

Raina groaned. "Just when I thought it was hope for you. He did!" She pointed to the ring on the table. "Literally proof." Raina looked down at a sleeping Sylar and kissed her forehead. "Sy, your mom's a goofy. I'm convinced."

"Shut up," Nicole said, rolling her eyes as she crossed her legs under her body. "I still feel like the way I found out wasn't right. Even if he didn't know she'd be there when he saw her he could have pulled me to the side or something. You know I don't like drama like that."

"I get it," Raina said. "But you'll figure it out soon enough."

Nicole was glad when Raina decided to go home. She loved her cousin, but nobody seemed to understand how Nicole felt.

Meeting that woman not even a few hours after he asked her to be his wife was like a slap in the face. There shouldn't have been anything another woman could come to tell her about her man that she didn't already know. He made her look stupid.

She sighed, trying to focus on things she could control. Sylar would be one in a month. Nicole was looking for a bigger place so Sylar could have her own room while also waiting on a job offer. She'd gotten a few interviews the last couple of weeks and that seemed to be the only thing keeping her from crying most days. She'd heard of a heart vs. mind battle, but it really felt like she had two hearts that were trying to stand on business.

One heart had been down this road. Had fallen for a man, took his word as bond and ended up crushed, only to will herself not to be bitter to the next man and go through it all again. That heart was tired of the hamster wheel that broken relationships had her on. That heart looked down at her baby girl and contemplated never trying for a romantic relationship again.

But the heart that belonged to Rashaad was still alive and well. That was the one that remembered that feeling of thanking God for the safety of her man's arms. The one who was almost always brought to tears at his thoughtfulness when he bought something for her and Sylar just because. The one that could relax because she knew her man had her back. That he loved her. The one who could walk around blindfolded and not worry about getting hurt.

Both of them made Nicole's head spin so much that she had no idea where she'd end up.

Her phone rang and she frowned to see it was her baby daddy.

"Hello, Julian."

"What my baby doing?" he asked. "Can I come get her?"

"You're asking today?" she asked. "How mature of you."

"I'm actually in the car, but I didn't start driving until I called first."

Nicole laughed. "I needed that laugh."

"You good, Nic?"

"You can come get her," she said, ignoring his question. "But can you bring her back tonight?"

"Tonight! Why don't you go chill with your man or something? I'll bring her back in a couple days."

"A couple days?" she mocked him. "It's not your weekend yet."

"We really arguing over who keeps this kid?" he asked. Nicole laughed. His comment about Rashaad wasn't lost on her, but she would not give Julian the satisfaction to know they weren't together anymore.

"A couple days is a lot, Julian. You still get her on Friday!"

He sighed. "Okay. The morning?"

Nicole rolled her eyes. "Fine." She hung up before he said anything else and tossed her phone back on the couch. She snuggled next to Sylar and smoothed her hair down. It was currently in two space balls on top of her head. "Now what am I going to do when you leave me, sugar baby? I guess I can start planning your party."

She decided to use the Sugar Babies candy as the theme for the party. She thought it was funny when she searched it and sites about how to find a sugar daddy came up. She made a note to make sure nothing on the party invitation said sugar baby just to be safe. About thirty minutes later, Julian had taken Sylar and Nicole decided to go to the gym. She knew Rashaad was at work, so she didn't have to worry about running into him. After a good cardio session, she went home and planned on staying in until Raina told her to meet her at Marie's house for dinner.

When she got there, she sighed to see her mother's car parked out front. If she hadn't already told Raina she was coming, Nicole would have turned around.

"About time," Simone said as Nicole walked in through the open kitchen door from the garage.

"Didn't know I was on a schedule," she said, holding up a bottle. "I bought wine."

"You never bring wine to my house."

"You don't invite me over," Nicole said. Simone's nose flared but she didn't respond.

"Okay stop, damn," Marie said, taking the bottle. "Y'all starting like kids already." Nicole wanted to tell her that her sister started it, but she left it alone. "Where's my baby?"

"Her daddy kidnapped her," Nicole pouted.

"You could have told him no," Marie teased. Nicole shrugged. She was honestly crazy about the relationship Julian and Sylar had. Even just playfully arguing with him about who got her that day was a blessing to her. She'd seen it go the other way too many times in life. Julian hadn't flirted or hinted at anything more with her since he finally confessed to being single so everything on that end was okay with Nicole. She didn't know if it would change once Julian found out she was single, but she'd cross that bridge when it was time.

"What's for dinner?"

"Salmon croquettes."

"And fried potatoes or mashed?" Nicole asked. Simone laughed.

"I asked the same thing."

"Here," Raina said, passing them both glasses of wine. "We'll open yours next. That's something new I wanted to try."

"You were serious about the wine thing?" Nicole asked. A few days earlier, Raina expressed an interest in becoming a sommelier. Nicole hadn't even heard of it until Raina mentioned it.

"Sounds so fancy, doesn't it?" Marie said. Nicole smiled. She always envied how even if the idea seemed crazy, Marie was always down to support her daughter.

"Sounds like something that costs a lot of money but don't make a lot of money," Simone said. Nicole rolled her eyes before sipping from the glass.

"This is good," she said. Raina nodded before making hers swirl around in her glass. She sniffed it before taking a little sip. Her facial expression made everyone laugh. It even seemed to put Simone in a less cynical mood. The majority of the night went well until after they were done eating and Rashaad came up.

"I can't believe all that happened," Marie said. "He seemed like a nice guy."

"Looks can be deceiving," Simone said. Nicole shook her head.

"He's been divorced," Raina said. "We all have a past."

"Lying about it makes it seem sneaky," Simone said. "And what real man really wants to take care of someone else's kid."

Everyone got quiet as Nicole shook her head, putting her wine class down on the table. "Let's just get this over with."

Simone frowned. "What?"

"Your real issue. You being mad Danny left you."

"Nicole," Marie said, trying to diffuse the situation. Raina cursed under her breath but only sipped on her wine.

"What does he have to do with this?" Simone said, turning to face her daughter.

"I get you're mad because your child got in the way of this wonderful man sweeping you off of your feet, but when are you going to get over this shit!"

"Watch your mouth!" Simone said. "You don't know what you're talking about."

"It took me a minute to put it together," Nicole said, smirking. "Why you kept shading Rashaad and pushing the fact that I should be a family with Julian. I had no clue what that was about especially since I told you how Julian treated me. Then it hit me."

Simone tried to keep her poker face but blinked away her tears. "It's been over 20 years since..."

"Exactly!" Nicole yelled. "So admit it. You're still salty because the man you thought would take all of your problems away told you he didn't want to raise another man's child! Admit it, Ma! Go ahead!"

"Fine!" Simone screamed. Raina gasped as tears streamed down Nicole's face. Marie just shook her head. "You want to hear it so bad, you're right. Because your no good ass daddy used to go upside my head every chance he got. He's been less than 20 minutes from you your whole life and still has nothing to do with you. A man finally loved me for me but because I took my momma and my sister's advice and didn't get an abortion, I was forced to choose you over love."

"Simone!" Marie yelled.

"No, auntie," Nicole chuckled, holding her hand up. "She's not saying anything I didn't already know. I just didn't realize she made all the things wrong in her miserable life my fault."

"You're damn right it's your fault! You walk around saying how you want to be married and have a family and not be like the rest of us. You act like you're so much better than us and here you are a single momma just like us! How does it feel?"

Nicole sighed before standing up, realizing this conversation wasn't going anywhere. She'd known it wouldn't, but she'd gone from mad to hurt and that wasn't a nice place for her to be in. She grabbed her glass of wine, finished it off before putting it down and grabbing her purse.

"You're right," she said. "I am a single mother like the rest of y'all. I realize now that life happens. I loved someone blindly that hurt me and that was my fault. I didn't take his hesitation to commit to me for what it was and that was my fault. I decided to keep my baby because I wanted her and if that was selfish, it's my fault. But guess what? None of that is hers. She didn't do anything wrong. And she has a mother AND a father who both love her and will always love her regardless of their relationship status. That's what keeps me from being a bitter baby momma like you were." She turned to leave but had one more thought. "And I had a man who loved me and my child! He loved me so much that he asked me to marry him. So men like Danny aren't God's gift to earth. He wasn't half the man Rashaad is and I'm sorry you didn't get to experience that. I really wish you would have so maybe you wouldn't hate your own daughter so much."

With that, she left.

chapter nineteen

Nicole focused on the computer screen as she read the beginning salary on the offer letter in her email. It would just about double what she was making now. She could get a bigger place. Sylar could have her own room. She would get a bigger kitchen and closet. It wasn't a work from home position, so she wasn't happy about that. However, she knew with her support system that everything would work out. Julian's mom and Pierre's mom had both already agreed to watch Sylar during the days since they were both retired. She would trust them over a daycare anyway.

She wanted to call Rashaad and tell him the good news. But it had been two months since she'd seen him. There were no more voicemails. No more roses delivered to the house. Nothing. It was time to move on.

She pushed that thought away as she drafted her resignation letter to her current job. Nicole frowned when she got an unexpected call from Sage.

"Hello?"

"Hey Nicole, how are you? It's Sage."

"I know," Nicole giggled. "I had your number saved from the party."

"Oh cool. Well, I was calling to see if you'd be interested in a modeling gig for Sylar?"

"Whoa," Nicole said from shock. Sage giggled. "She's cute and all but where did that come from?"

"One of my clients is opening a boutique for babies. I told her she needed a photoshoot. She has a toddler but needs a cute little baby girl, too."

"Aw, that's so sweet of you to think of her," Nicole said. "Send me the details."

"Really? Okay great! It was Pierre's idea. I'll make sure to negotiate a good rate for her and get it approved through you first."

"Rate?"

"It's a paid gig, baby. We don't do free in this family," Sage said. Nicole chuckled.

"I'm sure the college fund her daddy started will be thankful," Nicole said.

"Great..."

Nicole could tell by her tone that Sage wanted to say something else. "Was that all?"

"Actually no," Sage blurted out. "You know I'm not one for gossip but I overheard a conversation yesterday that you may want to know about. I don't know the type of relationship you and your man have, so you may already know."

Nicole frowned. "What's going on?"

Sage sighed. "Did Julian tell you Tessica broke up with him?"

Nicole chuckled. "Yes, he did. I hope he also told y'all how crazy he must think I am to want to marry him."

Sage groaned. "So it's true? He asked you that? Oh brother."

"I shut it down though," Nicole said.

"Apparently your man did, too."

Nicole froze. "Sage...what?"

"I heard P and Julian talking about it. I don't know where, but they ran into each other and Julian said they had words about it."

"When was this? What did he say?"

"That's all I know, Nicole. I'm sorry to even bring it up but I told P that Julian was wrong. They think it's noble to want a two-parent household but I said he should have thought of that before getting you pregnant."

Sage went on a mini rant about it, but all Nicole could do was wonder what happened. She knew Rashaad didn't say anything to her because they weren't speaking, but she had no idea how that conversation could have gone. Julian was a smart ass and she didn't see Rashaad taking too kindly to that.

"They didn't fight, did they?" Nicole asked.

"I didn't hear anything about it getting physical."

Nicole sighed, not even wanting to tell Sage that she and Rashaad weren't together. "Well, Julian hasn't fake proposed anymore so maybe he got the point."

"Yeah, well...I just thought you should know."

Nicole smiled. She could tell even with Sage's prissy attitude at times that she was a girl's girl. She didn't have to tell Nicole that at all. She appreciated that.

They talked a few more minutes before getting off the phone. Nicole looked over at Sylar who was toddling around playing with her toys. She always knew her baby was cute, but that was what all mothers did. Hopefully she'll act decent on the photoshoot. Sylar did not like to sit still for too long.

After drafting the letter, she got herself and Sylar ready to go to the gym. There was a Zumba class she wanted to go to and thankfully it was the hour before the gym daycare closed. They made it just in time for her to drop Sylar off and catch the end of the first song. After her workout, Nicole took a moment to stop sweating before heading to get Sylar. On her way to the door, she bumped into someone coming around the corner. He was so tall and muscular that she almost fell but he grabbed her elbow to steady her.

"That was my fault," he said. "You okay?"

"Are you a wall?" Nicole asked, gaining her balance. "Yikes!"

He laughed. "Don't do all that."

Nicole looked up at the sound of his laugh and noticed how fine he was. He had at least half a foot on her height with neatly groomed facial hair and a fade. His smile is what made her forget what she was doing.

"You good?" He asked, raising his eyebrows in question.

"Nicole," she answered. "Yes, I'm good."

"Cool. I'm Cody. I assume you're going in here?" he asked, pointing to the daycare. Nicole nodded before he opened the door for her to walk inside first. She immediately spotted Sylar laying back on one of the toddler chairs watching a movie. She went to sign her out and noticed Cody walking near her.

"Same type of time huh?" he asked, picking up a little boy who was also on the carpeted area. His little head fell straight on Cody's shoulder and his eyes closed.

"Aw, he's so adorable," she said while picking up Sylar. Her little hand smacked Nicole in her face as she went to kiss her cheeks, which was actually more of a bite. Cody and Nicole both laughed. "She's aggressive, obviously."

"He's fooling you right now with this sleep act," Cody said. They laughed before walking over to the cubbies to get their respective baby bags. "It was nice meeting you..rather running into you though. You mind if I get your number? You single?"

Nicole raised her eyebrow as she thought about the question. Was she single? She hadn't seen or talked to Rashaad in two months so technically she was. Was she ready to date again? Was this man even asking her all that? She sighed, deciding to just nod her head and not bombard him with all of her current feelings.

"Are you saying yes to being single or me getting the number?" he asked. Nicole blushed.

"Both."

He smiled again. "Cool."

Cody turned out to be a cool guy. They talked on the phone for a few days before meeting up at the gym again. Their first date was to the smoothie shop next to the gym. Nicole thought it was cute and somehow seemed to take the pressure off. He was a trainer and seemed very flirtatious, Nicole immediately noticed the women of the gym giving her weird looks whenever they interacted together. She also made note of how he talked about his son's mother. He seemed to work her into almost every conversation they had. Nicole wondered if he still had feelings for her or not, but since she wasn't heavily invested in whatever they were doing, she decided not to worry about it too much.

A few weeks later during one of their gym outings, Nicole almost tripped over her own foot when she saw Rashaad walk through the gym doors.

Outside of her occasionally checking his social media pages, she hadn't seen him in months. She had almost convinced herself that she was over him, but now that she laid eyes on him she knew that was a complete lie. As much as she wanted to be able to see him looking as heartbroken as she felt, it was the opposite. He looked good. His skin was glowing. His locs looked longer. She couldn't tell if he looked more toned or if it was in her head, but everything was working together for his good and she didn't like it one bit.

"Your time is up."

Nicole's head snapped back in Cody's direction. "Huh?"

"Your warm up is over," he chuckled. "Don't try to get out of this workout now."

Nicole groaned, almost forgetting she told Cody she'd do his back day routine with him. "I changed my mind."

He laughed. "Females usually do," he said. That made Nicole cringe, but she kept silent. "It won't be that bad." She froze when he tapped her butt, wondering if Rashaad noticed she was there and saw that interaction. "Let's get this work."

Nicole tried to focus on the workout but kept looking around to see where Rashaad was. He hadn't seemed to see her yet, but Nicole followed his entire workout. At first she was worried that Cody would notice, but he seemed preoccupied as well. Or he didn't care. She finally made it through his workout before he let her go stretch.

"We going next door?" she asked, which seemed to be their new routine. Cody nodded but looked around.

"Give me a minute."

Nicole frowned but nodded, continuing to stretch her hamstring as Cody walked off. She decided to go do a slow walk on the treadmill while waiting for him and that's when she finally bumped into Rashaad.

"Sorry," she said, trying to turn the other way. He moved to stop her. "I wasn't paying attention."

"I can tell," he said, looking down at her. "You seem busy with this nigga touching you the whole time."

Nicole looked up into his eyes and swallowed the saliva in her throat at his stone expression. "He wasn't touching me the whole time."

Rashaad shook his head. "I expected more from you."

Nicole stood up straight. "What? You seem to forget we aren't together because you lied about a whole wife. I'm single now. I can do what I want."

"I didn't lie to you and I know you're single but I still expect more from you than to mess with a nigga who ran through every woman at this gym."

Nicole couldn't say she was surprised or that she thought Rashaad was lying. It was evident in how Cody moved, but that wasn't the point.

"I'm not doing this with you," she said, trying to walk away. She gasped when Rashaad pulled her back to him and bent down to whisper in her ear.

"You don't gotta do nothing with me, but think about this and think real hard. You know the truth. You know how much I love you and your daughter and that I'd never hurt you intentionally.

You know the type of man I am and you know you want to be with me. You don't have too much more time to play with me. And unless you really want to be done and give up everything we had, let that be the last time another man touches you."

chapter twenty

"I don't know why I agreed to this," Nicole said. After she'd greeted the birthday girl and put her gift on the table, Nicole made her way to an empty seat and tried to stay out of the way. After being ignored by Rashaad for twenty minutes, she called Raina to calm her down. "He's really not even paying attention to me."

A few days after her run in with Rashaad at the gym, Nicole got an unexpected call from Shyann. She urged her to come to Miss Diane's birthday party that following weekend. Nicole tried to explain that she and Rashaad weren't together anymore. Shyann wasn't trying to hear that and said that Miss Diane personally asked for her. Nicole really thought about declining, but the truth was she felt good that his mom liked her enough to invite her to her birthday party. That, plus the fact that she wanted her man back meant she needed to be there. However, it was clear from the moment she walked in that her man would not make it easy.

"Did you expect him to just fall to his knees? This really the third time you played him," Raina said. Nicole huffed.

"You need to be on my side."

"And you need to get off this phone and get in the field," Raina teased. Nicole couldn't help but laugh at the social media reference. "But for real, don't be a rude guest. The family invited you so that means someone is on your side. Get your man back, cousin."

Nicole nodded even though Raina couldn't see her. She told her bye just as Ayden walked over to her. Nicole rolled her eyes.

"I come in peace," he said, holding up an unopened margarita can.

"Peace?" she said, snatching it. "Really?"

"That was my fault. I didn't know she would act like that and I didn't know you didn't know the situation."

"Why did you invite her?" Nicole asked.

"I knew Shaad wanted to see Imani," he said. Nicole softened at that explanation. "That was all I was trying to do."

She sighed. "I guess I can't be mad at that." Her words trailed off as she spotted him by the dj booth, leaning over to whisper something. She loved watching him interact with his family, she could tell he enjoyed it. His smile was wide and he laughed a lot.

"If it helps," Ayden said. "He misses you, too."

"It doesn't for real," Nicole admitted. "We don't have to miss each other at all."

Ayden shrugged in defeat before holding up his own can. Nicole playfully rolled her eyes before knocking her can against his and opening it to take a sip.

After the conversation with Ayden, a few drinks and some food, Nicole loosened up a little. A few of Rashaad's family members that she'd met a while ago began to come in so she had a few people to talk to. Imani was there as well, fortunately without her mother. She made it a point to come and speak with Nicole.

"I just love your hair," she said, twirling one of her locs around her finger before quickly moving back. "Oh I'm sorry! I didn't ask. Do you mind me touching your hair?"

Nicole giggled before she nodded. "That was nice of you to ask."

"Momma tells me you're always supposed to get permission to touch somebody and nobody has the right to touch me without my permission."

"Your mom is right about that."

"I saw a picture of your baby at daddy's last weekend. She's so cute. Where is she?"

Nicole's heart jumped. "She's with her dad."

"Aw, I wish she was here so I could play with her. I love babies."

"You have any siblings?" Nicole asked. Imani shook her head.

"Nope. Just me."

"You bothering Miss Nicole?"

She closed her eyes a little at finally hearing his voice. Even though he wasn't talking to her, she missed him saying her name. However, she was irritated that he'd only decided to come speak to be nosy. Imani giggled.

"I'm not bothering her," she said before turning to Nicole. "Right?"

"No you aren't, you're actually keeping me company since I'm here by myself."

Obvious to the shade, Imani smiled before scooting closer to Nicole. She hadn't much experience with teenagers, but Imani seemed like such a sweet little girl.

"Did you eat?"

Nicole looked up and realized he was finally addressing her. She didn't answer him, only looked over his features before turning back to Imani. She asked her about the cartoon on her shirt and that sent Imani into a tailspin of stories. Nicole heard Rashaad chuckle before he walked off.

The sunset and the kids seemed to disappear, turning the party from family friendly to a turn up. The music got a little louder and the drinks got stronger. Nicole was determined to leave after finishing her last drink. She was tipsy at this point and knew that she was close to embarrassing herself if she didn't leave soon.

"Nicole! Come play spades," Miss Diane said. "My son needs a partner."

"She can't play for real," he said, not looking up at her but shuffling the cards. Nicole huffed before turning from the drink table and headed their way.

"I can," she said, not wanting to remind him that he taught her.

"Let's see what you got, niece," Shyann said. Nicole sat in the folding chair and scooted in silently. She looked at Rashaad, waiting to see if he'd look up at her but he was determined not to. The energy at the table shifted, but Miss Diane and Shyann were either too drunk to realize or were trying to keep it from getting awkward. Nicole let Rashaad bid the first two hands before she cleared her throat.

"You said I can't play but you seem to be the problem."

"Oop!" Miss Diane said. "Son, you ain't tell baby girl that your momma was a spades champ."

"You just worry about your hand," he said, his nostrils flaring a little.

"Is that all I need to worry about?" Nicole blurted out, fed up with whatever game they were playing. "You ain't even looked at me long enough to realize what's on my damn hand."

Rashaad's eyes zoomed in on the engagement ring that was back on Nicole's left hand. She watched his Adam's apple move as he swallowed his saliva and finally made eye contact with her.

"What's that mean?"

"You know what it means! Why are you being so mean to me right now? I didn't do anything to you."

"You left me!" he said, slamming his cards down. "Again. That's all you seem to know how to do. Every time some shit don't go your way you up and leave."

"That's not fair," she whispered, trying not to cry.

"I get me not telling you about Chanel and Imani was wrong, but I deserved for you to at least hear me out. Not leave me for months and have another nigga in your face at the place you know I be at.

"I didn't do anything with him," Nicole admitted.

"You better fucking not have," Rashaad snapped.

"Shy, let's give them a minute," Miss Diane said. Shyann groaned but followed Miss Diane away from the table. Nicole bit her lip and tried to hold her emotions in. She didn't want to do any of this. She just wanted her man back.

"You got me out here blind, Nicole," Rashaad said, defeated. "Everything I did, every feeling I have for you is real. You told me you felt safe with me, that you loved me."

"I do…"

"Then why you got me out here blind?" he asked, throwing his hands up. "How am I supposed to believe that if I can't see it? What's stopping you from believing that yourself?"

The tears fell despite her best efforts to keep them in. That was the same question she'd been asking herself for weeks. Before she would have blamed it on past failed relationships, her non-existent relationship with her dad and her dysfunctional relationship with her mother. Nicole knew all of those things were true, but they didn't erase the facts.

"I can't even give you an excuse, baby," she said. "I don't even think there's anything I can say that you would believe at this point. I was wrong. I know I was wrong about how I handled it and we didn't operate like that. I should have let you explain because I know you have my best interest at heart but I'm sorry. All I can say is if the offer still stands, I want to be your wife. I want to grow with you and thug it out with you." The grin on his face felt like a reward to her. "And I promise not to run again. I may go off, get mad, and react irrationally…but I won't run."

"Can you prove it?"

Nicole frowned a little but nodded. "How would you like me to prove it?"

epilogue

"Can we talk?"

Nicole wasn't sure what her mother wanted at that particular time, but she had been cordial with her up until that point. The road to this day wasn't easy for them, but looking over her reflection in the hotel suite's mirror made it worth it.

She'd been untraditional, letting her man pick out her wedding dress. He was against it at first, but their compromise was he wasn't going to see it on her until she walked towards him at the altar. Her locs were up in a petal design on top of her head, held up by a crystal, white gold crown. Her dress was mostly satin and clung to her shape, but the straps were a petal design that matched the design going down her back. It accentuated her waist and hips but flowed from there. She was all dressed and ready with Raina taking candid photos of Sylar and Imani while the actual photographer was downstairs with Rashaad and Ayden.

Sylar's dress was a big Cinderella style with the same petal design as Nicole's with a bow in the back. They left her wild curls out and she refused to put her shoes on. She was a very assertive and confident 2 year old now and didn't do anything she didn't want to do. She had taken to Imani almost immediately. Now that Chanel seemed to let her come around more, it was a no brainer for Nicole to include her in this special day.

That night at Miss Diane's birthday party when Rashaad asked Nicole to prove that she wouldn't run anymore, he made her set a wedding date. She'd chosen the day they matched on the dating website. Rashaad was a little upset that it was a year away, but they made another deal that seemed to appease him.

Nicole glanced at her mother and sighed. Since their blow up last year, their relationship had been strained. Nicole was cordial with her and still tried to involve her in the wedding planning process, but she really didn't want to have this conversation on her wedding day.

"Can it wait?" Nicole asked Simone. "I think they're almost ready."

"I just checked," Marie said, standing next to her sister. Nicole sighed before turning to her mom.

"I really don't want any negative energy today. Can we just..."

Simone waved her hand while shaking her head. "I wanted to apologize. Didn't want to start your marriage off without it."

Nicole blinked, waiting to see if any smart remarks would follow. Raina cleared her throat as Marie suggested they give them some privacy. She picked Sylar up on her way out as Imani followed behind them.

Simone looked around the room before her eyes settled on her daughter and she smiled. "You look beautiful, baby."

"Thank you."

"I'm sorry things didn't pan out with your dad."

Last year when they really started planning the wedding, Nicole reached out to her biological dad. One thing that Simone was right about was him being so physically close. Nicole used to wonder why he didn't want anything to do with her but after a while she decided to let it go. That argument with her mom bought back up some old wounds. She wanted to try and mend their relationship and hopefully have him walk her down the aisle. It didn't work out as planned.

"That's not your fault."

"It is," Simone said. "That relationship was doomed because of how we ended and I'm sorry I didn't take you into consideration with that. It was why I pushed so hard for you to be with Julian, but I was wrong about that. Rashaad is a good man for you."

Hearing his name calmed her. "He's a great man for me," she whispered. "God sent."

Simone nodded. "I see that and I'm grateful that you have that."

Nicole took a second before nodding. "Thank you. I appreciate that."

A knock on the door was followed by Raina peeking back in. "They're ready for you, Mrs. Baptiste."

www.ingramcontent.com/pod-product-compliance
Lightning Source LLC
Chambersburg PA
CBHW071957170626
46813CB00005B/1909